NIGHT CREATURE

Look for all of the books in

THE WEREWOLF CHRONICLES

trilogy:

Book I: *Night Creature*

Book II: *Children of the Wolf*

Book III: *The Wereing*

THE WEREWOLF CHRONICLES

NIGHT CREATURE

Rodman Philbrick and Lynn Harnett

AN
APPLE
PAPERBACK

SCHOLASTIC INC.
New York Toronto London Auckland Sydney

No part of this publication may be reproduced in whole or in part, or stored in a retrieval system, or transmitted in any form or by any means, electronic, mechanical, photocopying, recording, or otherwise, without written permission of the publisher. For information regarding permission, write to Scholastic Inc., 555 Broadway, New York, NY 10012.

ISBN 0-590-68950-9

12 11 10 9 8 7 6 5 4 3   6 7 8 9/9 0 1/0

Printed in the U.S.A.   40

First Scholastic printing, July 1996

For Erica Engel

RULES OF THE WEREING

1. A werewolf is created by birth or bite.

2. The wereing is the change from human to beast and lasts for the three nights of the full moon.

3. The first wereing of a werewolf child occurs in the twelfth year.

4. If the werewolf child makes a kill in the three nights of the full moon, it shall have all the powers of a full-blooded werewolf and remain a monster forever.

5. A full-blooded werewolf can change into human form at any time, but must become a werewolf when the moon is full.

6. A werewolf cannot cross water.

7. A werewolf cannot tolerate anything silver.

In the Beginning . . .

I am a monster. Listen and I will tell you how the wereing began, and how I was raised by wolves, and what happened in a place called Fox Hollow.

Fox Hollow. To all appearances a perfectly ordinary town filled with perfectly ordinary homes and perfectly ordinary people. But appearances truly are deceiving, because Fox Hollow is not ordinary. Oh, no.

Something terrible crept into the town and changed the people who lived there. Something so monstrous, so terrifying, that you may never sleep again. . . .

Me.

In the beginning was the wereing. The change that comes for the three nights of the full moon and turns me into a howling beast. The change that waits in my blood and cannot be denied. The change that makes me a night creature — a werewolf — a foul thing who lives in the darkest part of the shadow, waiting for prey to come within range of my glistening fangs.

I know nothing of my mother and father,

save that they, too, must have been were-wolves. How they came to leave me in the woods I do not know, but anything is possible. They might have been chased by hunters, or attacked by other night creatures. Or maybe I was stolen from their lair — but why any creature would want to steal a wretched beast like me remains a mystery.

The first thing I remember is the smell of warm fur. The fur of the Wolfmother who took me into her den, and fed me with her litter of cubs, and protected me from the terrors of darkness even though I didn't look anything like the other wolves.

Oh, how I remember the warmth of that den, the feeling of <u>safeness</u> as we snuggled together. The low <u>rrrrrrrrr</u> sound coming from our throats meant we were happy, and the Wolfmother <u>rrrrrrrr</u>'d back at us and licked our faces to make us clean.

For the longest time I thought like a wolf, ate like a wolf, ran like a wolf, bayed like a wolf at the light of the moon. The Wolf-mother's cubs were my brothers and sisters and I loved them and played with them and fought with them.

I thought I was a wolf. Until the wereing began . . .

x

Chapter 1

The day my life changed forever I was feeling sorry for myself.

There I was lying on my back in the clearing outside our den, letting the two cubs tumble over me. Leaper and Snapjaw nipped at each other, making happy little growling noises in their throats as I rubbed their fur.

I loved the cubs, but it wasn't fair that I had to stay near the den while the rest of the family went hunting. They hadn't left me behind because I was such a great cub-sitter. No. The other wolves thought I was a useless hunter.

Slow, weak, and useless, like the cubs I was minding.

I was about twelve years old and I'd been with the pack for almost nine winters, near as I could recall. And still I had to rely on the other wolves to get me food. But how did they expect me to learn how to hunt if they left me behind every time?

"Gruff!" barked Leaper. "Gruff! Gruff!"

Gruff, that's me. Wolfmother named me for the first sound that came out of my mouth, and now little Leaper was trying to get my atten-

1

tion. I growled and she backed off, puzzled, and began to whine.

Sighing, I longed to be out in the woods with my throwing stick. I was getting so good I could knock a leaf off a tree. Any day now I'd actually hit something we could eat. That would show them!

For some reason I was jumpy and more moody and I couldn't concentrate on anything for more than a minute.

Did I have some kind of premonition — a feeling about what was going to happen? Maybe even then, before the Change came, something inside me was stirring, trying to get out.

"Ow!"

That's what I got for not paying attention. Leaper had gotten overexcited and buried her teeth in the base of my thumb. She didn't break the skin — she knew better than that — but those sharp baby teeth still hurt.

I shook my injured fist in her face and she quickly backed off. Crouching low to the ground, the little cub rolled to show me her belly. That was her way of apologizing.

Naturally my heart melted like snow in the sun. I reached over to scratch her belly, burying my hand in the thick soft fur. She wriggled in the dirt and growled contentedly while I looked around for Snapjaw.

Snapjaw — he had a bad habit of biting everything in sight, although nobody but me seemed to think it was a bad habit — was sitting on his haunches with his head thrown back. His little black nose was twitching like crazy. He was sniffing at the air as if he could taste it.

Which he probably could. He had an awesome nose. It was hard to keep him near the den as he was always following some new scent into the woods.

But not this time. Rump high, the cub backed slowly away from the forest. The slate-gray hair began to rise along his back in stiff peaks.

Whatever was out there, Snapjaw wanted no part of it.

Behind me I heard a low growl. Leaper was up on her feet, her ears pointed toward the forest, twitching anxiously.

Something was wrong and the cubs knew it.

The hairs on the back of my neck rose. My eyes scanned the trees anxiously but I couldn't see anything, and I couldn't hear or smell danger as well as the cubs could.

Snapjaw suddenly bolted. Leaper was right behind him. The two cubs disappeared into the safety of the den.

And then I finally heard it, too.

Strange noises from the swamp, like some big animal was moving around.

But there weren't any big animals around here except for us.

CR-ACK! A big branch broke. Leaves crunched. This animal, whatever it was, was moving slow. But coming closer.

Twigs snapped under heavy feet.

I suddenly realized what had me spooked. The thing out there didn't care who heard it coming. It wasn't afraid of anything, not even wolves.

The noises stopped. Had it gone away?

I was listening so intently I forgot to watch my back. That's lesson number one. The first thing a cub learns. And I forgot.

There was no sound. Just a gray blur of motion on the edge of my vision as it sprang out of the forest.

I threw up my hands to ward it off but too late.

OOF!

The full weight of the huge beast slammed

into my back and threw me to the ground. Rank-smelling breath was hot against my bare neck. Knife-sharp teeth grazed my ear.

Then the great jaws opened and I saw the gleam of teeth just as they sank into my throat.

Chapter 2

It was Wolfmother.

I tried to cry out but the big wolf held my throat between her jaws. Her teeth were hot needles against my skin. Fear churned in my belly. What had I done?

Then I understood — the strange, noisy creature was still out there in the forest and Wolfmother was making sure I kept silent. She was guarding the den and her cubs.

SNAP!

Danger was coming closer. I could feel Wolfmother tensing, her jaws still clamped around my neck, as if I were a noisy cub. I tried to tell her with my eyes that I understood, that she could trust me not to make a sound. But she wouldn't let go.

Then at last, when I thought my whole body would seize up in one big cramp, she lifted her head, keeping her paws on my shoulders. Her eyes bored into me. It was only when she saw me press my lips tightly together that she released me. She twitched her ears once toward the noises still coming from the woods — closer now.

Then with a switch of her tail she let me go

and hurriedly checked on Leaper and Snapjaw. Once she knew the cubs were safe, she stood at the entrance to the den, narrowing her eyes in the direction of the mysterious noises. She bared her teeth, growling low.

I hurried to Wolfmother's side and crouched next to her. I made the reassuring yips that told her I would keep danger away.

She turned her eyes to mine and gazed at me.

"Grruff," I growled, telling her, don't worry, Gruff will protect you.

In reply she gave a short, sharp bark, urging me to hurry.

Chapter 3

Our den was in the drier portion of a forested swamp, rich with game animals and thick with trees and low thickets.

I knew the swamp like I knew my own hands and moved stealthily, sliding my feet so as not to crunch the leaves and pine needles, ducking under branches rather than pushing them out of my way, avoiding mud holes and wet places.

I moved without making a sound.

CRUNCH! CRASH! THUD!

Ahead of me the beast floundered around like it didn't care who could hear it coming. I shuddered to think how huge and ferocious it must be.

I circled around its strange noises and then began to creep back toward it from behind. If it got too close to the den I'd get it to chase me instead.

I could do that much for my wolf family after all they'd done for me.

SNAP!

I froze, holding my breath. Lost in my thoughts, I had stepped on a dead branch.

But the strange beast just came crashing on. My skin crawled. What kind of animal was so fearless it didn't care how much noise it made?

Then the creature made a strange sound. My scalp prickled. I felt like lightning had just shot through me, zapping my arms and legs. Suddenly I wanted to run back to Wolfmother. But the new sounds tapped a beat in my head, drawing me closer.

I forgot to watch my feet, stepped on a twig, and blundered through a pile of dead leaves. But I wasn't worried about that now. I was close. Excitement churned my stomach. But what should I do?

THWACK!

Something slashed through the leaves faster than sight and buried itself in a tree trunk no more than an inch from my nose. Something deadly — and wonderful!

Chapter 4

I dropped to the ground as another thing whistled through the air. It hit a branch over my head and dropped to the ground in front of me. It was a stick thing, with feathers on one end and a sharp point on the other. What was it, and how did this strange beast make it fly?

"I got it!" cried a voice. "Let's see if it's dead."

A voice like mine! But this voice made strange high babbling sounds all strung together. The sounds echoed in my brain, somehow reminding me of long ago, of the time before Wolfmother took me into her den. And then something really strange happened.

The sounds began to sort themselves in my mind as if something deep inside me was struggling to make sense of the odd Legwalker noises.

And then suddenly I understood that the creature had tried to hit me with the sharp stick thing. He thought he had killed me.

"You didn't hit anything," said a second voice. "You couldn't hit a train if it was right in front of you!"

"Oh yeah? Then you go check it out if you're

so sure there's nothing there. I'm telling you, Billy, I heard something big moving around in those bushes. I bet I hit it right through the heart!"

There was a silence. My heart raced. I could almost understand them. It seemed as if I'd heard the sounds they made with their mouths sometime long ago. I felt sure I could understand more if I only had more time to listen and remember.

I understood the other animals who lived in our swamp. They all had their own cries of greeting and warning and fear. But this was different.

It was like some big part of me was waking up after a long sleep. It was wonderful, exciting. But it was scary, too.

"They're your arrows," said the one called Billy. His voice sounded shaky. "You go check it out."

"All right. I'm going."

One of the creatures began moving through the bushes in my direction. I tensed. What should I do?

I couldn't let them catch me.

But if I tried to run they'd shoot more of those sharp flying things after me. Besides, I wanted to hear more. I wanted to see them up close. I wanted to know why I had never seen or heard them before.

As the creature stumbled blindly through the undergrowth, I crouched, hiding behind a tree. My hand closed over a good-sized rock.

"Yuck!" the boy cried. I heard the sucking sound that meant he'd stepped in a mud hole.

"What was that?" said the other one, Billy. There was fear in the breathy sound of his voice. It calmed me — they were even more scared than I was.

"I don't know. Probably nothing." He grunted, pulling his foot out of the mud. "This place gives me the creeps."

Billy sounded frightened. "I think we better forget about those arrows and get out of here, Paul. I have a bad feeling about this."

"I can't! They're brand-new arrows," said the one called Paul. "My dad just bought them for me." Hesitant steps crunched toward me again. "It's probably just a squirrel or something."

The smell of their fear was thick in the air. But the one called Paul was coming closer. I had to keep him from finding me. I threw back my head and opened my throat, letting a picture of Wolffather Thornclaw grow in my head until I felt I was him.

Then I howled.

12

"Arrrrrooooooooooh!"

When I lowered my head I could hear them crashing and splashing through the wettest bog in this part of the swamp. I stood quickly, hoping for a good look at them. Although they moved slowly, stumbling into mud slicks and holes, tripping over tree roots and snagged by brambles, they were already almost hidden among the trees.

But I could see what I already suspected. They were Legwalkers, like me!

My own legs itched to follow. I wanted to know more. Where had they come from? But I sensed somehow it would be dangerous to get too close to these creatures. Torn between doing what I wanted and doing what I should, I bent to pick up the sharp stick — the *ar-row* — off the ground.

What a strange weapon! How did it work? I reached for the one stuck in the tree. It didn't move. I tugged harder. It stayed stuck.

I dropped to my knees, and using both hands, worked the thing back and forth until it finally came free. I stared at the hole in the tree, excitement swelling in my chest.

Now I *had* to go after the Legwalkers! This arrow weapon made my throwing stick look like cub's play. It had taken months to shape

13

my throwing stick and sharpen it and learn how to throw it so I could hit something.

How had those two clumsy Legwalkers made this marvelous arrow fly fast enough to bury itself into the tree? I had to find out.

The creatures were crashing through the bog, away from me. I began to run silently after them. They had secrets I wanted to know. Secrets that would make me as good a hunter as a wolf.

Chapter 5

It didn't take me long to catch up, despite all the time I'd wasted. They had stopped running and were stumbling along, out of breath.

"That was really weird," said the one called Paul. He had a curved piece of wood slung over his shoulder — the arrow shooter.

"Maybe we should go back," said Billy.

"Go back? Are you crazy?"

"What if it was somebody's dog you shot?" Billy had a worried look on his face.

Hidden in the trees, I peered at them through the leaves. I felt they were talking about me and thinking of going back. How could they not be more scared by my ferocious howl?

"It didn't sound like any dog I ever heard," said Paul. His arrow shooter caught on a branch and yanked him backward. "Ow," he said, easing it off his shoulder. "I don't see how the Indians ever sneaked through the woods carrying a bow," he said. "It snags on everything."

"Had to be a dog. What else could it be?" Billy insisted. "There's nothing in these woods bigger than a squirrel."

Paul had the bow in his hand. "Maybe it was

a wolf," he said. "My dad said there used to be wolves in this swamp."

My pulse quickened. Suddenly I saw how I could get the arrow shooter for myself. Once more I threw back my head and howled.

"Arooooooooooh!"

Both Legwalkers squawked in terror and took off running. Just as I'd hoped, Paul dropped his bow.

I snatched it up and disappeared again into the trees. I loped off toward the wolf den, stopping every once in a while to try out the bow and my two arrow things.

I was acting foolishly, I knew, but I was so delighted with my new weapon it never occurred to me the young Legwalkers might come back. With bigger Legwalkers, carrying bigger weapons.

No, I never suspected that my carefree days were about to end, or that the horror to come would swallow up not only the innocent wolves, but the Legwalkers, too.

Chapter 6

But I wasn't worried about the Legwalkers, or how meeting them would change my life for the worse. I was too excited by my new weapon, and by seeing the Legwalkers.

I was puzzled, too. How could the Legwalkers look like me but be so different? They wore odd bulky skins on their bodies and didn't know anything about the woods. And they made those strange fast noises. Other animals communicated when they needed to — a bark or a screech or a short call. But the Legwalkers made their sounds all the time, even when there was no danger or food to call attention to. And how could it be that the noises seemed familiar to me?

As I loped along, heading back to the den, I tried making some of the sounds the Legwalkers had used. But even though I could hear their strange words plainly in my head, I couldn't quite get my mouth around the sounds. They were too complicated, not at all like growling, barking, and howling.

Excited by my thoughts and at how far and fast the arrows would go, I lost track of time. It was nearly dark by the time I reached the den.

17

I stashed the bow and arrows with my throwing stick in some bushes. It was silly, of course, but I didn't want my wolf family to see my new weapons. I felt embarrassed about them. The wolves didn't need that kind of help when they hunted. And on that great day when I returned from the woods with game for the whole family, I wanted them to marvel and wonder how I'd done it. They would praise me and share the food I'd caught — I'd be as proud as Sharpfang, the best hunter in the pack.

My wolf family were all gathered together in the clearing. The cubs were scrapping over a piece of meat. When Wolfmother saw me she raised her head and growled in annoyance, so I knew she'd been worried.

"Grrruffff!"

I growled to reassure her that I was all right and the danger was gone.

I wished I could let Wolfmother know about the Legwalkers, but probably she already knew. The wolves knew lots of things that I didn't. I had to see things with my own eyes, but they used their ears and noses to keep track of just about everything that happened in our swamp.

My brother Sharpfang growled impatiently, and only then did I notice he was guarding a kill. I was embarrassed and ashamed that I hadn't noticed it sooner. Any self-respecting wolf would have smelled the fresh meat long before he arrived at the clearing.

I barked enthusiastically and ran around him in fast circles, trying to make up for my mistake.

Big and silvery gray, Sharpfang walked around his prize, strutting and preening a bit before dragging a haunch to Wolfmother and then bringing a second haunch to me. It was a deer — fresh venison. He and Thornclaw had obviously fed deeply before bringing back what they could.

The two proud hunters watched contentedly as the rest of us ate.

As darkness fell, the wolves stretched out on the ground, too full to move. Even the cubs, Leaper and Snapjaw, were quiet for once. I lay down, resting my head on Sharpfang's flank.

A rush of love swept over me for my wolf family. Why couldn't I always feel this content? They accepted me with all my shortcomings, why couldn't I accept myself?

And then it began. The horror that would change me forever.

Drowsy, I snuggled against my wolfbrother and was beginning to slip into a light sleep when I felt a strange tingling in my hands. At

19

the same moment, Sharpfang stiffened. He stood up so suddenly my head bounced against the ground.

I sat up, rubbing my head, growling questioningly.

The moon was rising over the tops of the trees. It was a full moon, big and yellow, and as the light fell on my face, I felt dazzled. The silvery light was so beautiful. For a second everything between me and the moon seemed to vanish.

A rustling, scampering nose brought me back to myself.

The wolves were all on their feet. Wolfmother's eyes were like hot yellow stones. Thornclaw's eyes were shadowed, but I could see a hard gleam. Sharpfang's eyes were wide and blazing.

They were all staring. Even the cubs were staring at me. And they were afraid. . . .

Of me.

Chapter 7

Leaper and Snapjaw suddenly backed away from me, yipping in fear.

Wolfmother chased them into the den and stood in the entrance, solid against the night. She made a strange whimpering noise.

I whined loudly, asking Wolfmother what was wrong.

Starting toward her, I signaled that I wanted to play with the cubs. I rolled on my back to show how unthreatening I was.

But Thornclaw darted at me, snapping. I scuttled backward, away from the den.

What was going on? What had I done?

Behind me I heard a deep growl. I whipped around. Sharpfang was standing there facing me. His hair bristled along his back, stiff and coldly silver in the moonlight.

I barked at him, thrusting my face at him in a way that demanded he look at me, Gruff, his own wolfbrother.

He snarled viciously, the sound building from deep in his broad muscled chest. Sharpfang dropped back onto his powerful haunches, ready to attack.

My head buzzed so I could hardly think.

21

Then I realized there must be something awful behind me. Some threat so big it could scare all the wolves at once.

I looked over my shoulder, but there was nothing there. Nothing that I could see.

I looked back at Sharpfang. His jaws were open and his teeth shone wetly in the moonlight. Still snarling, he was crouched to spring. His tongue flicked over his teeth. His jaws dripped with rage.

My own jaw dropped in horror.

It was me he was going to attack. Me, his own brother.

Sharpfang was about to tear me limb from limb.

Chapter 8

I barked at him frantically, holding my puny hands out as if that would stop him.

As panic shot through me I stumbled to my feet. My only hope was to surprise him, duck under his attack and run.

As if I could ever outrun any wolf, much less Sharpfang.

But as I rose up, Sharpfang yelped. He dropped out of his crouch and ran, his tail hanging low, weird frightened sounds coming from his throat.

"RRrrufff!" I barked as he fled the clearing, trying to call him back.

My mind was spinning in confusion. The tingling in my arms and legs was growing stronger, making me want to run and howl. I didn't know if I felt good or rotten.

But a secret part of me was pleased to see Sharpfang run from me with his tail between his legs.

I looked toward the den. Thornclaw huddled beside Wolfmother, his muzzle to the ground. I growled at him. "Grrrrrrrr!" as if *I* would do the attacking from now on.

What was happening to me?

I had to get out of there before I did something I'd really be sorry for.

I barked loudly and ran off into the swamp after Sharpfang. He was long gone, but I kept running anyway, full of churned-up feelings and strange, scary questions.

How could my family turn against me like that?

And where did that hard, mean feeling swelling up inside me come from?

I chased after my wolfbrother but couldn't find him. After a few minutes I realized I was totally alone in the swamp. The woods were silent. There wasn't so much as a frog croaking.

But something weird was going on — I'd come a long way and never even stumbled in the dark or put my foot into a mud hole. And I wasn't even slightly winded.

The tingling was stronger in my arms and legs. The strange thing was, it no longer felt unpleasant. It was like an electrical current flowing through me, lighting me up from inside.

I threw back my head, feeling the moonlight on my face. I'd never noticed before how cool and smooth moonlight felt on my skin. As I stood there drinking it in, the moon grew brighter, bathing me with energy.

I felt so strong I wanted to roar. The buzzing in my head had stopped. My wolf family seemed far away, part of another life.

I knew I could do anything.

I breathed deep and the whole swamp entered my lungs.

R-I-I-I-I-I-I-P!

The sound startled me. I looked down to see my animal-skin coverings bursting open and falling away from me.

My muscles bulged and rippled, writhing under my skin. I was turning into a monster.

Chapter 9

Part of me knew I should be terrified. There were pains like sharp stones stuck between the bones of my joints, but I brushed off the pain like I would a fly.

I dropped to all fours suddenly, as if I'd been grabbed. The bones in my arms cracked and shifted, then a louder *CRACK!* and my legs bent in a new way.

Power surged through me like a tumbling flood. The power was greater than any pain. I watched new muscles ripple down my arms and thicken my fingers. Lean muscles stretched along my legs and I felt the urge to run — for joy.

But the Change wasn't over yet. My face twisted like rubber, my teeth grew long and pointed, and my tongue stretched to fill my new jaw. I ran my tongue along the rows of razor-sharp teeth.

My skin thickened and hair sprouted, becoming a kind of fur although not thick and pearly like my wolf family's coats.

My ears grew longer and more pointed and filled with the sounds of the night. Suddenly I could hear the heartbeat of a rabbit frozen with

26

terror in its hole. And I could see an owl at the top of a tree, crouched motionless behind the leaves.

And my nose! I could smell Sharpfang's fear, far away to the west. I could smell the leaves and the water and all the animals in the forest swamp.

My nose was a miracle. Just by scent I could follow the trail of every creature, tell where it had been and even where it was going. Nothing could escape me.

I had become a wolf!

Only better.

I threw back my head, feeling the moonlight flow over me. I stretched my jaws wide and let out a howl of joy that shook the leaves off the trees.

I'd become a monster, and I loved it.

Chapter 10

I howled again, feeling myself at the center of the world. The sound could be heard for miles. I knew it would drive a chill into the bravest heart and I swelled with pride.

But howling wasn't enough, there was a hunger in me, too. I prowled through the woods, scaring even the ants out of my path. I wanted something. But what?

Hunger gnawed at me. My nose quivered. Every creature in the bog shrank from me.

The rabbit, cowering in its hole!

Saliva dripping from my gaping jaws, I clawed frantically at the ground, desperate to reach the hiding rabbit and devour its tender flesh.

The creature huddled into the earth and didn't try to escape. It had already given up, resigned to its fate.

But suddenly I stopped. I stood motionless, my mind in strange turmoil. Something was terribly wrong — I had already eaten! I had a full belly, and wolves don't kill when they're not hungry.

Revolted, I looked down at my hairy limbs. No longer Legwalker, not quite wolf, what was I?

The wonderful joy that coursed through my veins like liquid light turned sluggish. My muscles itched to be running, my teeth longed to sink into something warm and solid. But my stomach churned with disgust.

Part of me wanted to race through the swamp, part of me wanted to hide somewhere safe, like that rabbit. As I twisted in confusion the moon caught my eye. I threw back my head and howled mournfully.

"Arooooooooooooohh!"

As the lonely sound died away, a snickering laugh came out of the darkness. Something was there. Something that wasn't afraid of me.

I whipped around. But although I could see the tiny birds huddled in their nests and sense the moles quivering in their burrows, I saw nothing that might have made that awful laugh.

"*Aaoooww,*" howled a raspy, mocking voice out of the dark. "*Aaeeeiiiihh!*"

But inside my head the horrible howls became words like the Legwalkers spoke, only whispery and irresistible.

"*Follow me, little one, and you shall learn who you are!*"

Chapter 11

Leaves rustled. Something moved, and then the shadow of a shape bounded off into the swamp.

I leaped after it, the moonlight flooding my body with energy. I ran like the wind, and all living creatures scuttled out of my path.

The strange, shadowy creature drew me on, but I never caught more than glimpses of it. The beast loped on all fours and had a hunched, hulking appearance. Its head looked large and misshapen — like nothing I'd ever seen before.

"Aeeiighh!" it howled. But inside my head it sounded like *"Follow me! Follow me and find the truth!"*

Deep into the swamp we went, deeper than I had ever been. Wisps of steam rose from murky pools and dead trees made crippled shapes against the night sky.

My hunger grew, clawing at my belly, but it never occurred to me to stop. I couldn't stop. Running fed the hunger and the swifter I ran, the stronger I became.

Heat rose off me in waves so hot I warmed the wind. And the wind itself began to speak to me, whispering its admiration. *"Little one,"* I heard. *"Run little one, run to us. Come, little one!"*

Whatever was happening to me, it made me strong, stronger than I'd ever been. I cleared a pool of muddy water in a single bound. This was the way I was meant to be — swift as the wind, more powerful than the strongest wolf.

Suddenly a tree in my path changed shape and I shied away, startled. Something flashed red eyes at me. I glimpsed a sharp-fanged grin, and then it was gone. That was no tree. Or was it? I swept the woods with my magical eyes but there was nothing there.

"Little one," sighed the wind. *"Come to us!"*

My pace faltered again as I realized those voices were not the wind at all. From everywhere the whispering voices came at me, howling softly, menacingly, pulling me deeper into the wettest, most dangerous part of the swamp.

"Follow," the voices urged me. *"Follow deep into the swamp. Follow and find the truth!"*

The air around me grew heavy with the smell of rotting things and stagnant water.

I began to see flickering red eyes, glowing for an instant, then gone. Twisted shapes loomed up out of the muck and when I looked, they disappeared. There were strange night creatures all around me and I couldn't see them!

But they could see me.

Ragged shreds of laughter caught at my ears.

It was an evil, mocking sound.

As it filled the night I realized I was running right into the thick of them.

But I couldn't stop.

Chapter 12

"Heeeeeeee-heeeee-heeee! Look at what happened to poor little Gruff! Haaaaaa-haaaaa!"

The laughter came from all sides. I was surrounded.

Strange, monstrous forms flickered around the edges of my vision. But when I tried to focus on them, they turned back into shadows. Baring my teeth, I snarled at them to keep away from me.

I splashed into a mud pool, spattering myself with horrible-smelling muck. The mud sucked at my feet. I lifted one foot and felt the other sink deeper. I couldn't get free!

As I struggled, the mud pulled me in slowly. Suddenly I could smell all the other creatures of the swamp that had stumbled there and were imprisoned in the mud forever.

I panicked, struggling wildly. All around me the laughter grew louder, mocking my terror.

"What's wrong, little Gruff?" said a cruel voice in my head. *"What are you afraid of?"*

Red glowing eyes watched me from the darkness. The night creatures were creeping closer and closer as my useless struggles drove me deeper into the ooze.

I growled threateningly, trying to force them back.

But the red glowing eyes came closer.

I felt a cold touch on the hairs of my belly. Mud! I was still sinking. I forced myself to be calm. I knew how to get out of this if I would just think. But the night rustled with hunched shapes and whispery shadows. Cruel red eyes stared at me, cackling with evil pleasure.

I sank another inch. Think! I closed my eyes and pictured myself getting free. It was almost too late.

I took a deep breath and heaved myself over onto my side. With a loud *POP!* an arm and a leg came free. I rolled over, pulling with all my might. The rest of me popped free! The mud pool sighed and subsided.

As I lay there panting, the red-eyed night creatures crept closer, closer. They weren't laughing now. They whispered to one another, making a sound like tree limbs grating together in a gusty wind.

The moon slid behind a cloud and hid them. For a few moments they were just humped black shapes against the night. Except for those red eyes glowing like hot coals. Red eyes in the night, staring at me.

The hairs stood up along my back. I jumped to my feet and tried to run away. But wherever I turned, the monstrous shapes were there.

Closer they came, closer and closer.

Their breath stank worse than the swamp mud that covered me. The strange, shadowy creatures smelled of death.

A snarl started deep in my throat and I bared my sharp-fanged teeth.

The moon sailed out from behind a cloud and suddenly I could see them! I sucked in my breath. They were werewolves!

Horrible creatures with matted hair and snarling faces. Part wolf, part human, and one hundred percent monster. Monsters so ugly and terrible it made my belly churn with sickness. Their long, pointed fangs glistened in the moonlight. Between patches of straggly hair their skin was like half-rotted bark. Their gnarled feet and hands were tipped with long yellow claws.

But their eyes were worse than anything. Those hot red eyes burning with a fever for blood!

Their ugly-sounding whispers came into my head. *"Come with us, little Gruff. Come with us and learn the truth."*

I backed away, snarling louder. Inside I was quivering with fear. My mud-covered fur bristled threateningly.

"GRRRRRRRAAAAAAA!" I snarled at them to get away.

Instantly all of those eyes became narrowed slits, shooting bolts of red fire. The creatures raised their terrible claws and gave out an ear-splitting shriek that meant, *"You belong to us!"*

Then they hurtled straight at me, fangs dripping. The forest shook with their stampeding feet. Hundreds of claws aimed directly for my eyes.

The night creatures — the werewolves — were going to rip me apart!

Chapter 13

I crouched, cringing in terror.

But I felt the power flowing into my haunches. I jumped, and the force of my muscles lifted me up, over the heads of the shrieking beasts. Their questing claws just missed me.

When I landed, I found myself clinging to the swaying branches of a tall tree. Scrambling up higher, I perched at the top, my chest heaving.

"There he is! In the tree! Get him!"

Below me the pack of night creatures gathered around the tree, peering up. Their piercing red eyes found me easily.

They snuffled and whined below me. *"Why do you run, little one?"* they taunted, their uplifted faces grinning horribly. *"What are you afraid of?"*

I shuddered as their voices sifted up through the tree, making the leaves shiver.

They began to scrape their claws against the bark. *"You are one of us!"* they howled inside my head. *"Come down and let us show you the way of the night!"*

I shuddered, trying to shut out the snarling sounds — and that's when I happened to notice my hands, grasping the branch in the cool moonlight.

My fingernails had become sharp yellow claws that dug into the tree branch. My feet, too, curled around the branch in a way no Leg-walker or wolf feet could. But my claws were long and graceful, not scabbed and thick like theirs. And my feet were smooth, not gnarled.

Long hair covered my powerful arms and legs and my wolflike chest. But even covered with mud it was silky looking, not wiry like the night creatures.

Maybe I was a monster, but I wasn't like them! I wasn't. I wasn't!

I looked down at their burning eyes. Their long misshapen arms waved at me. They jumped from foot to foot on bowed, ugly legs.

They were horrible, evil! Nothing like me.

I shut my eyes, not wanting to see them. What did these twisted, red-eyed beasts want with me? I just wanted to run, find my wolf family, and show off my new power. I would never be like these disgusting creatures of the night. Never!

I kept my eyes screwed tightly shut, hoping they'd tire of taunting me and go away.

And after a while the low snickering laughter and sneering calls did stop. I started to breathe easier. Maybe it was all a dream. I was asleep, and when I woke up I'd be just Gruff again.

Then the air whooshed!

Something large landed right beside me on the branch.

Chapter 14

The branch barely quivered, but the swampy death smell of the creature nearly knocked me off my perch.

Don't look, Gruff! I told myself. Don't look and it will go away!

I kept my eyes closed. It had to be a dream. A horrible nightmare.

A growling sound made my ears twitch. Then I realized the thing beside me on the branch was laughing quietly to itself. It was a soft, evil sound.

The evil laughter chilled me to the marrow.

It was laughing at me as if it could read my thoughts, as if it knew exactly what I was thinking!

I heard a slithering sound and then something cold and slimy touched me. I jerked away and started to fall. Teetering, I opened my eyes.

Inches away, red eyes burned into me.

"You are mine!" it said inside my head. *"Mine, mine, mine!"*

The horrible creature grinned at me. Saliva dripped from its teeth. Somehow I knew it was the same werewolf that led me here into the swamp.

I opened my mouth to scream and all that emerged was a hissing sort of growl. I had to get away! Without thinking, my feet let loose of the branch.

I fell.

A gleeful howl rose up from below.

Too late, I remembered the night creatures gathered down there.

I was dropping right into their wide-open jaws.

Chapter 15

Faster than a striking snake, a long arm shot out of the dark and gripped me.

I dangled motionless, high above the ground.

Soft laughter, dripping like venom, came from above me as shrieks and growls of disappointment erupted from below.

I moaned in fear, unable to escape. The werewolf claws were icy cold but somehow burned into my arm. Slowly, it pulled me back up to the branch where it crouched.

As the thing growled, words dropped into my brain, hissing like hot coals spattered with rain. *I am called Ripper. Don't try to get away from Ripper, little one.* The creature's stinking breath choked me as it pulled me close. *You cannot escape!*

The thing laughed again and released my arm. Even though it was no longer holding me, I could still feel its grip burning and stinging.

I looked at my arm. My skin bubbled under five slime trails left by the claws. And at the end of each slimy burn was a mark, curved like a half moon. Small red dots appeared at each tiny wound.

I stared in horror as the dots of blood swelled.

"*You have nothing to fear,*" the creature called Ripper purred in a soft, oily voice. It was trying to sound kind and soothing, I realized.

But something dark was dripping from its claws. Blood. My blood.

"*You must come with me,*" Ripper said, absently raising a clawed hand to its face. As I watched, it licked the red drops with a flicking tongue.

"*Mmm,*" it said, glowing eyes half-closed in pleasure. "*Your blood is delicious, but too thin.*"

Then its eyes snapped open and bored into mine. I couldn't look away. "*You will come tonight and make your first kill. Then the wereing shall be complete.*"

It slurped up the last drop.

The — the wereing? What did it mean?

"*The wereing is the change from human to beast,*" the creature explained, although I had made no sound. "*Our blood runs in your veins. You are one of us. I know you feel our power.*"

I wanted to shake my head no, but the creature narrowed its eyes menacingly and revealed long, slavering fangs. "*Under my care you will learn to kill,*" it growled. "*Once you have made your first kill, the wereing will be complete.*"

The creature leaned closer. I could smell death on its breath. It purred deep in its throat and said, *"Taste blood in the light of the full moon and all the powers of the night shall be yours."*

Inside me the strange gnawing hunger quivered. What was wrong with letting this creature teach me how to hunt? I wanted to learn to hunt for my wolf family, right?

I liked my new power, didn't I?

Without warning, the thing called Ripper grabbed my hand. Even as the slimy touch turned my stomach, the creature's power sent a jolt through me that made all my hair stand on end.

In the next instant we left the branch and sailed through the night.

Chapter 16

Our powerful spring from the tree took us over the heads of the creatures below. We landed softly and the rest of the beasts fell in behind us, slobbering and fighting and howling for blood.

"Follow me and you will be safe," Ripper reassured me.

He began to run like the wind and I kept up with him easily.

Why had I thought him evil? I wondered. He was graceful and swift and obviously very wise. I should be flattered he took an interest in me.

Who was *I*? Nobody. But someday I might be as powerful a leader as he was, the great and terrible Ripper.

A cold pit of unease stirred inside me. Was the werewolf using my brain to tell me what to think?

I threw off the thought with an impatient shrug. Ripper was going to teach me to hunt! That was what I should be concentrating on, not silly ideas that came out of—well, wherever they came from.

Feel the touch of the wind and the glory of the moon, I told myself. Enjoy this special,

magical power and don't spoil things with fool-
ish worries.

The hunt was the important thing. And why
shouldn't I be excited about my first kill?

My brother Sharpfang had made his years
ago. And now he was grown, while I was still a
cub dependent on my family for all my food.
Perhaps once I'd made my first kill I, too,
would be an adult.

Maybe that was all that was meant by "the
wereing." I had nothing to fear, right?

Right?

"ARRROOOOOOOHHHHHHHH!"

The howling werewolves invaded the bog,
leaping murky pools, snapping trees in half,
slinging mud at each other, driving the
swamp's animals from their safe homes.

And I invaded with them, grinning as a
frightened raccoon scampered up a tree and
a doe huddled shivering over her fawn. Bats
skittered across the moon, screaming in terror. An opossum fell terrified from its
perch. The thunder of our passing shook the
ground.

My new blood sang in my veins with the
thrill of the hunt.

Then, jumping over a muddy pool, I saw my reflection in the rippled surface and I stumbled in horror.

The wavery image burned itself into my brain. I was starting to look just like them! Like the ghastly night creatures!

My pace faltered and Ripper screamed at me to run. But where were they going? What did they really want me to do?

I remembered what the hideous creature had said: *"Make your first kill and the wereing shall be complete."*

My new body urged me to forget about thinking and just run and run. The monster part of me hungered to stay with the night creatures and howl at the moon.

But now I knew Ripper had been inside my mind, trying to make me think like he did.

"Noooooooooo!" shrieked Ripper, sensing my doubts. He gnashed his fangs and snapped viciously as his hold on me loosened and fell away.

Deep inside, I was still Gruff. And I knew if I gave in to the hunger I would be like these night creatures forever.

At that moment a heavy cloud slid over the moon. Now was my chance!

In the cover of dark I slipped away, into the shadows.

The werewolves didn't see me go and I got a good head start, running as fast and as silently as I could. I didn't know where I was going, only that I had to get away to save myself.

Too soon, the cloud passed. As the moonlight fell over the night creatures, they realized I was gone.

"Little one! Come back! Come back or die!"

Their howling fury froze my blood.

I hadn't got very far away. Their senses were even keener than mine and any second they would find me.

Even as the thought entered my mind, Ripper scented me and turned the snarling pack in my direction.

They were right behind me, catching up fast!

I couldn't escape.

Chapter 17

Moaning in fear, I kept running.

Behind me the creatures were crashing through the swamp, gaining on me.

Desperately I looked for a hiding place. But where could I hide where they wouldn't sniff me out? It was hopeless.

The moon glinted on a pool of water in front of me. Water! Maybe that would work!

Steeling myself against the cold, I slipped into the stagnant water. If wolves couldn't smell their prey in water, maybe werewolves couldn't, either.

It was my only hope.

The mud slithered under my feet. My head dipped below the surface, and I came up sputtering. I froze, hoping the night creatures hadn't heard.

The slithering voices came out of the night.

"Little one, are you there? Little one, come back, come back!"

Peeping up from my watery hiding place, I could see their red eyes gleaming in the dark. They were snuffling at the ground nearby and coming closer.

Silently I swam to the thick roots of an old

cypress tree and huddled there, shivering in water up to my neck. The slimy roots helped hide me. The water smelled of mold and muck and drowned animals.

The stench made my eyes water but it was still better than the hot stinking breath of those evil night creatures.

"Where is he?" they hissed to each other. *"Can you smell him? Can you?"*

They searched for a long time, rooting at the ground and lifting their noses to sample the air. Glowing red eyes pierced every corner of the night.

The werewolves moaned and shrieked and cursed.

"Get him! Find him! Make him one of us!"

I stayed absolutely still as the dank coldness of the water seeped into my muscles. I was stiff with cold, sick with fear.

After a long while, the one called Ripper began to call. His angry howls formed words inside my head and banged against my skull.

"Little one, you can't escape your nature. You cannot escape us!" Anger made his voice crack and hiss inside my head. *"The curse is in your blood. You cannot resist! Come out and we will show you how to take a kill!"*

The others howled and stamped the ground

and echoed his call, shrieking, *"Little one, little one, come out to us!"*

The beast in me yearned to come bounding out of the nasty water and run with the pack. What harm could it do? It was my nature! I must celebrate my nature!

But the part of me that was still Gruff refused to give in — I wouldn't kill, no matter what. I stayed hidden in the icy pool. The cold crept deeper into my bones. I ached and felt I'd never be warm again.

Hours passed and still the grisly things searched, rattling the trees, snarling in anger, and calling to me with pretend sweetness in their foul voices.

Hiding under the old swamp tree, I didn't move. I could no longer feel my arms and legs. I was nothing more than a wretched lump. Never in my life had I felt more cold and miserable and sick in my heart.

I was a monster who didn't want to be a monster, and it was killing me.

Chapter 18

I woke up with a jerk.

My body was numb from the neck down. I couldn't feel a thing.

But it was quiet in the swamp. Somehow I must have slept. Or passed out.

I opened my eyes. Dawn. The terrible night was over at last. I sagged in weak relief against a cypress knee — the root of the cypress tree that sticks up out of the water.

I looked around cautiously.

"Aack!" I jumped.

A frog sat on a rock an inch from my face. It stared at me for a moment, then blinked slowly and slid out of sight into the water.

A few birds sang in the tops of the trees — which they would never do if the werewolves were still lurking. I was safe at last.

Slowly I crept to the shore. I braced my hands on the solid bank to heave myself out and gasped at what I saw.

My hands! They were my own again, small and hairless, with pale, grimy nails and no claws.

I pushed myself onto dry land and lay there panting, feeling the warmth of the sun on my shivering skin. I touched my face and looked carefully at my arms and legs.

It had worked! The monster inside me was gone and I was plain little Gruff again.

As miserable as I'd been, hiding in that cold swamp water, that's how happy I was now. It had all been worth it. I was free!

I started to get up, hearing my bones creak and groan, when a sound made me stop in my tracks.

A howl.

The birds scattered and another frightened frog plopped into the water.

"ARRROOOOOOOOOOOOOOOOH!"

The howling filled the air, died away, and rose up again.

It was heading my way.

Fast.

Chapter 19

A large gray shadow flickered among the trees.

I stumbled to my feet and tried to cry out. But my voice was a croak. And my legs still wouldn't work right. I couldn't move.

The howling started again, calling to something deep in my blood.

Soon it would catch my scent. I didn't want to be found helpless like I was.

Forcing myself to my feet, I staggered in among the trees. I was starting to get some feeling back in my muscles when I stepped into a mud hole and went down hard.

"Aargh!" I dragged my foot clear, relieved to find I hadn't sprained it.

Then, as I turned, a huge gray blur filled my vision. It hurtled through the air right for me. I put up my arms crosswise to shield my face from the impact.

"Oooomph!" I was knocked flat to the ground and the air whooshed out of me.

A long, warm tongue lapped at my skin, running along scratches and cleaning off the last of the mud. "Wolfmother!" I barked happily. Her rough tongue tickled.

After she'd satisfied herself that I smelled basically the same and was not too damaged to walk, she stood at my side and barked at me to follow her. We were going home.

So that's what I did. It took most of the day. We were a long way from the den, plus I was sore and bruised, and branches and stickers kept snagging my bare skin.

Wolfmother led me to the spot where I'd left my deerskins but there wasn't much left of them to put on.

It wasn't until we got to the den that I really felt like my old self again. Snapjaw and Leaper jumped all over me to show their joy, and Thornclaw motioned for me to finish his dinner.

Only Sharpfang kept his distance. He watched me with cold eyes and moved away whenever I approached, keeping to the edges of our clearing.

"Rrrr-rrrr," I growled pleadingly, crawling closer to him.

I rolled over and put my chin to the ground to show I was friendly and harmless. But Sharpfang was having none of it.

Saddened, I let him alone and played with the cubs until the sun began to go down.

And then I remembered something that sent an icicle right down my spine. It was something the night creature Ripper had told me. Grinning his horrible grin, he had snarled gleefully, *"The wereing takes place over the three nights of the full moon."*

Only one night had passed.

I looked up as the sun dipped below the trees. Night fell quickly.

And the full moon was about to rise again.

Chapter 20

I had to leave, at least for the night. I couldn't let anything happen to my wolf family because of me. Feeling sad, I slipped out of the clearing, away from the den. Only Sharpfang saw me go and he turned his back when I caught his eye.

Maybe nothing would happen this time. I hadn't made my first kill, despite all the urging from the night creatures. Maybe that meant the wereing was over for me.

But even as I thought these things the tingling in my arms and legs started again.

The moon was just coming up.

It happened faster this time. Strange, awesome power surged through me like an electrical current. My body changed, growing stronger muscles, fangs and claws, and matted hair. I dropped to all fours, my fur skins falling to the ground, a growl starting deep in my throat.

Above me, a family of baby robins cheeped in a nest as their terrified mother flapped away. A sleeping snake woke and slithered off into the cold mud. I could hear everything alive, right down to the heartbeats.

I was a monster again.

I began to run through the night, my muscles

flexing and stretching with pleasure. But this time the joy was spoiled by the thought of the night creatures. If I didn't hide soon they would find me. And this time they wouldn't let me escape.

If they got me tonight they'd make me kill in the moonlight, whether I wanted to or not. And that would make me a night creature forever.

I ran like the wind, faster than the birds that fled before me. Deeper into the swamp I went, deep into the bog, following my nose. I found my old hiding place, slipped into the water, and ducked beneath the cypress knees.

I was safe. If the werewolves followed my scent, they would lose it here. Maybe they'd think it was last night's scent they'd tracked.

Shivering in the icy water, I felt alone in the world, and hopeless.

The hours ticked by. Was I wrong about the night creatures? Maybe they'd forgotten about their "little one."

But sure enough, when the moon was high overhead, the foul beasts returned, snarling and screeching. They trampled the mud around my pool, snapping at each other in frustration.

"Little one, we know you are here," howled

the one called Ripper. *"Once you have tasted blood you will not want to escape us. Come out, little one, come out!"*

His cries hammered at my soul. I longed to leap out of the cold, murky water and join the night creatures in their dancing and howling. The power in me hungered and yearned and battered at my insides.

But I couldn't become one of them. I wouldn't!

Just before dawn the creatures melted away and I finally fell asleep.

This time the sun was higher in the sky when I woke up as plain little Gruff again. A weakling who was glad he hadn't turned into a night creature forever.

Off in the distance I could hear the "Ooooooooh!" howl of Wolfmother calling me back to the den.

When I finally dragged myself back to the only place I'd ever called home, Wolfmother was there to greet me. She rubbed her furry coat against my chilled skin to warm me and whimpered that she'd been worried.

I crept into the den and slept most of the day. Leaper and Snapjaw curled against me, nipping at my ears to wake me for play. But I was too tired.

One more night of the full moon. I shuddered to think of it. Warm as the den was, I still shivered with cold. But after tonight, I would be free.

Sharpfang woke me with a growl at sunset. He skipped out of reach when I tried to pat him.

This is the last night, I told myself as I trudged away from my family into the swamp.

Already my bones ached at the thought of more long hours hiding in the deep chill of the muddy pool. But it was the only way to make sure I didn't end up a monster forever. For some reason the other werewolves wouldn't enter the water even though I could. I knew I was safe there.

But that night I never made it to the safety of my pool.

Chapter 21

Darkness fell and at first nothing happened.

No tingling in my hands and feet, no jolt of energy. Maybe two nights was enough? Could the wereing be over?

I kept on, deeper into the swamp. But it was harder going as an ordinary Legwalker, without special powers and strength. Branches whipped at my face and roots kept catching at my feet.

It was so dark I couldn't see a foot in front of me.

Dark. Of course! My heart sank. The moon was rising later. The wereing wouldn't start until the light of the moon touched me.

I tripped in a mud hole and banged my knee on a rock as I went down. Dejected, I sat on a tree stump, rubbing my knee, noticing that all the normal night noises of the swamp had stopped.

I looked up just as the first rays of moonlight penetrated the trees. The shooting pain in my knee suddenly vanished. There was no tingling this time, just the rush of energy.

The wereing. It was happening!

Huge muscles roped my arms and legs, stretching and puckering the skin. Shaggy hairs sprouted on my back, chest, and belly. Curved claws sprang from my fingers. What was I so scared of? — it was *great* being a monster!

I threw back my head to howl at the moon. It seemed to shine for me alone.

As the satisfying howl died away, I breathed deep, tasting the richness of the swamp. The trees were outlined in silvery light. The night was mine.

"Arrooooooooooooooooh!"

The faraway chorus of bloodcurdling howls reminded me of what I had to do. I had to hide myself in that miserable pool until the moon set and the wereing was over.

But I hesitated. This was the third night of the wereing, my last chance to experience my new power. And besides, I wasn't like those monsters of the night, right? I was beautiful, my body strong and sleek.

It was the night creatures who were evil and ugly, not me.

Why should I hide in a muddy pool, miserable and shivering, when I could be racing the wind and tasting all of life in the air?

Because, said my Gruff-self, glum and practical, if I didn't escape the wretched werewolves, they would make me one of them. Ignoring my raging heart, I pushed the desire for freedom out of my mind and set off for the hiding place.

"Aroooo-rooo-rooooh!"

The horrible yowling of the monsters grew louder with every step. They were right in my path! Listening carefully I could hear them dancing in a circle in the darkness. My ears picked up a splash and suddenly I knew what had happened.

The werewolves had discovered my hiding spot and had it surrounded! If I tried to get to the water they would capture me. Besides, what good was the muddy pool if they knew about it?

The wild part of me leaped in the air for joy. Whatever happened, it wouldn't mean another night of freezing with nothing but my tormented thoughts for company.

The Gruff part of me was only a tiny voice in the vast night. The little voice kept saying there were lots of other pools in the swamp and that only in the water would I be safe from the powerful senses of the night creatures.

But the wereing had taken hold of me. I wasn't thinking like Gruff, but like the werewolf he had become.

The swampy wind felt delicious, ruffling my

fur, and the moon bathed me with cool light. The night beckoned me to taste all it had to offer — for one last time.

I turned my back on the slavering night creatures and began to run in the opposite direction. They'd never catch me. I could outrun the wind! Faster and faster I went, my feet scarcely touching the ground. The moon filled me with magic. I cleared trees in a single graceful leap and the grassy bogs were no more than puddles to me. I never even got my feet wet!

To keep out of the clutches of those monsters, I could outrun the moon.

The only thing I couldn't outrun was myself.

Chapter 22

In no time at all I came to a place in the woods I had never been before. The ground was drier and I could sense all sorts of creatures who lived here. I started to feel even more excited — a whole new world to explore!

I sniffed carefully but found no sign that any of my wolf family had ever been here. Why? It was a perfect hunting ground. I would bring them here, I thought proudly. This was my discovery!

I sat on my haunches a moment, sad that my family couldn't be with me on this wonderful night. If they could only see, they wouldn't be frightened, they'd be proud. I was no monster like those other beasts. I was magnificent!

Leaping straight up into the air, I landed high in a tree for no reason except it felt so good.

I looked back toward my home. But though I could sense Wolfmother curled around the cubs in the den and Thornclaw and Sharpfang prowling the edges of the clearing nervously, even I couldn't actually see that far.

I swung around on my branch to look the other way — the way I was heading. And what I saw there surprised me so much I almost fell out of the tree.

In the distance mysterious lights twinkled, like stars fallen to earth. But where the lights were, there was no swamp, no woods.

The swamp came to an end! Never having left it, I hadn't thought about what might lie outside our swamp. I just figured it went on forever, some parts boggy and dangerous, other parts dry and covered with trees.

What magical place was this?

One light, brighter than the others, drew me. It was like a beacon, shining just for me.

But instead of jumping from the tree, I climbed down slowly. I had to go to the light, I could feel it tugging at me. But I was frightened, too. What could it mean, twinkly lights out here at the edge of the swamp?

Could this be where stars were born? A little whine rose from my throat. That would be magic even too great for me. I hesitated. Maybe I should come back another night with Wolfmother. She would know what to do.

Growling at myself, I shook off these useless thoughts. Wolfmother had never been here before, my nose could tell me that much. And, as a puny Legwalker, it would take me half the night to reach this place, if I could even find it.

I ruffed out the fur along my shoulders and stood tall. What did I have to be afraid of? I, a being so powerful that all the creatures of the swamp fled the instant they sensed me.

Lifting my head, I howled at the moon. Its light poured down my throat, energizing me from within.

I began to run toward the light.

The ground was a blur under my feet, and the light grew brighter and brighter. It winked and sparkled at me, almost calling out for me to run faster, come quickly!

And then, as the trees began to thin, and odd bulky shapes loomed, the light grew so bright, it dazzled my eyes. I wanted to get up close to it and let it pour into me like moonlight.

The forest began to thin out until, finally, there were no more trees. The swamp ended.

I had come to the place of sparkling lights.

I slowed, slipping into the shadows, my ears twitching. Suddenly I heard a strange noise, like nothing I'd ever heard before. A thumping, rhythmical noise. The hairs along my ears prickled. I felt a shiver down my spine.

The mysterious sound was doing something to me, stirring me inside. It made my heart beat faster.

I moved closer.

Beyond the trees, out in the open, were things I'd never seen before. Huge, square-looking things. The things seemed to be made of pieces of wood. Light shined through square holes in the wood. And out of one of these giant things, the sound was coming.

Suddenly the sound stopped. In its place came a voice, which spoke to me, making Leg-walker sounds.

"Come on down!" it commanded. "Hurry now for the best prices!"

I didn't know what *pry-ces* were, but the voice made me feel eager to find out.

I obeyed the voice and stepped out of the safety of the swamp, into the light.

Chapter 23

My body felt horribly exposed out in the vast world with no trees to hide me.

Quickly I ran for a patch of darkness beside the nearest of the giant wooden things. My nose filled with hundreds of alien smells, things I had no names for.

I looked around in amazement. Many of the big wooden things had lights shining from inside — and in some of them I could see Legwalkers. These must be the Legwalker dens! But so many of them!

Whichever way I turned I saw more of the wooden dens, arranged in rows side by side. And all of them were so big. How many Legwalkers lived here? Each den was big enough for a pack of twenty, maybe thirty.

My mind boggled. So many wolves could never live together. There wouldn't be anywhere near enough hunting territory.

The Legwalkers must live more like bees than like wolf packs, I thought. They must make their own honey and have no need to hunt for food. I was glad the wolves had found me. I wouldn't want to live in a hive with millions of other Legwalkers!

But I couldn't help being curious. And the sweet noise coming from the nearest den still drew me. I gazed up. It was coming from a lighted square at the top of the den.

All of the dens had these square holes. The holes were covered with some kind of hard see-through material. A word came into my mind, a word from the distant past: *windows*.

So far none of the Legwalkers seemed to have seen me or sensed me. Suddenly I felt overwhelmed at the thought of being in the midst of so many of them.

The hair bristled up all over me and I shrank deeper into the shadows, my eyes darting every which way.

Did they all have bows and arrows? If one of them looked out and saw me, they could shoot me with an arrow before I could dive for the trees.

My stomach churned.

I might have left then, gone back to the swamp where I was happy and safe. But the wonderful sound coming from the lighted square suddenly got louder. The jangly, frantic pulse of it gripped my heart.

I had to get up there — had to see what was making that noise!

But as I lifted my head toward the lighted square, a chorus of alarm erupted.

"Ark-ark-arkark-ark!" Howling, yapping, and yipping noises came from many of the wooden dens. I could sense that the noisy animals were like harmless cubs, but they were frantically calling the Legwalkers to come with their dangerous weapons.

I pressed myself against the side of the den. There was nowhere to hide. The din of barking hurt my ears.

I could smell the confusion of the Legwalkers. Their noses were useless but they kept these tame creatures in their houses to warn them of danger.

Inside the dens, Legwalkers began to shout.

Doors opened.

I was strong but not mighty enough to fight off the Legwalkers' arrows.

Any second the Legwalkers would have me surrounded.

The trees were too far away.

My muscles clenched with fear.

The first Legwalker came rushing out of his den.

Chapter 24

I flattened myself against the wall of the den.

At first the Legwalker was alone. Staring out into the night but not seeing me — his eyes were too weak. Then another Legwalker emerged from a den on the other side. "See anything, Ed?" he called out.

I curled into myself, trying not even to breathe.

"Nah. Probably a fox from the woods. Everything seems quiet," said Ed.

"We had raccoons in the yard last night," said the other one. "I thought Misty would bust a gut barking."

"The dogs aren't used to living so close to the woods yet," said Ed. "Seems anything will set them off. One starts yowling and they all go crazy."

"Right. Another week or so they should be used to this place and settle down. Meanwhile, it's pretty nerve-wracking." The Legwalker laughed and started back to his den. "Well, good night, Ed. Let's hope that's all the excitement for tonight."

In the dens all around, Legwalkers were shouting at their animals to stop their noise.

The smell of the animals' confusion and fear was overpowering, but eventually they quieted down and stopped barking.

After a little while, I felt safe enough to think about the light coming from that one particular den. The strange, wonderful noises had started up again, drawing me closer. I had to get up there! I had to see what was inside that light, what made that marvelous noise!

All around me were dangerous Legwalkers. And their animals quivered with loathing and fear of me.

But I was going to find a way to get to that light. Or die trying.

Chapter 25

It was too high up for me to reach in a leap. The wall I was huddled against was part of a smaller structure with a low roof.

Inside the structure was a large dark thing with wheels and a sharp unnatural smell. The thing wasn't alive, but it had this smaller den all to itself.

Something about it nudged my deep memories of that time before the wolves. Some sort of fast moving blur. Another word came into my mind: *car*. But the rest of the buried memory wouldn't come.

I growled in annoyance and immediately the animal in the next den started yipping and whining again. The hair on my neck stood stiff.

In a panic I gripped hold of the wall and found I could easily leap to the lower roof. I scurried across and lay flat just in time.

The Legwalker banged out of his den again. Irritation rose off him in waves. "Okay, you kids, knock it off!" he yelled into the night and went back inside, banging the den opening again.

After that it was easy. I scrambled up the wall until I was on a level with the lighted window. Then I began to move sideways, like a spider.

I had to keep myself pressed to the wall and the going was slow. Suddenly I realized that if the Legwalker came out again, he couldn't possibly miss seeing me.

A sweat broke out on my brow and my pulse began to race. Anyone could see me here! But I was so close.

A scratchy, secretive sound close by startled me. I froze, my stomach curdling with fear.

The awful scratchy sound stopped.

I whipped my head around and as my hand moved, my long claws scraped against the wall. I almost laughed, I was so relieved. The scratchy noise was nothing but my own claws.

I came to an empty, darkened window. Curious, I cautiously leaned over to peer inside.

A horrible monster stared out at me! It showed horrible yellow teeth.

I lost my grip.

My claws skidded, scrabbling for a hold as I slipped.

The monster scowled at me, baring huge, dripping fangs.

Its eyes glowed ferociously.

There was a werewolf inside the den!

Chapter 26

I managed to stop myself before I fell to the bottom. Clinging with all twenty claws, I looked up.

The window was dark and blank. Empty.

Then I understood. I shrank back in horror. I had seen — myself! It was my own reflection in the window, just like I'd seen in the pool the first night.

Shaking, I felt sick. I hung on the wall weakly, not caring in that moment who saw me or what happened to me next.

But slowly the sound from the lighted window drifted down like sparkles in the air, soothing me. It wasn't like anything I'd heard before, but it called to me, filled me with longing. It was sweet and zingy and raw and thumping. Another long-forgotten word came into my head: *music*.

I breathed in and my nose filled with the distant smells of my swamp along with the exciting new scents I wanted to explore.

I shook myself, feeling my smooth pelt ripple. That monster couldn't be me! I wasn't evil! It must have been some trick of the material these Legwalkers used that made my reflection look so horrible.

I began to climb again, inch by inch. The lighted window was almost in reach. I pulled myself up very slowly and carefully and peeked in.

And almost lost my grip again! The Legwalker inside was the same young one that shot the arrow at me.

Cautiously I raised my head and looked again. Like a rush of tumbling water, my heart beat with strange feelings.

The Legwalker was sitting on a long soft-looking thing, his feet dangling over the edge. One foot bounced in rhythm with the sounds that had drawn me to him. The sounds were coming from a small brown box that sat on a flat structure with wooden legs.

The room was filled with warm light.

The magical sounds of the thing called music came to an end and a tinny-sounding voice — the same one that called to me at the edge of the swamp — began to speak.

"That was a blast from the past, folks — Aerosmith! And now for something a little more contemporary."

Again the musical sounds began and the Legwalker nodded his head to the beat and tapped his feet, too.

He was eating something sweet-smelling that instantly made my fangs drip with saliva. And he was turning the pages of a flimsy-looking thing filled with colorful pictures of monsters! Although the creatures in the pictures weren't as hideous as the night creatures, they were pretty scary. But the boy seemed to enjoy looking at them.

The den-room itself was breathtaking. There were shiny things everywhere. My fingers itched to touch them. Everything was so colorful and new and clean.

I wanted to be part of this wonderful place.

The Legwalker could be my friend. Maybe his light and his special magic noise box had drawn me here for a reason.

It looked so warm and safe in there. Maybe the Legwalker would be like my wolfbrother Sharpfang, who shared with me and was almost always ready to play.

What was the name the other Legwalker in the woods had called him? Paul, that was it!

Eagerly, I reached up a claw to scratch on the square and get Paul's attention.

Chapter 27

But just as my claws touched the glass, a section of the Legwalker's den-room opened.

Another young Legwalker came in — a young female. She seemed to be almost the same age as the one called Paul, only she had long brown hair swinging down to her shoulders.

She said something to Paul and he reached out and touched the sound box. "Okay, Kim, I'll turn it down," he said. Instantly the lovely sounds got quieter.

I didn't like that. But when she smiled, she had such a friendly look about her.

Kim spoke to Paul again and he laughed. They looked so happy together it made my heart ache with warmth.

The female Legwalker wrinkled her nose and made a face when she saw the monster pictures Paul was looking at.

She turned away and started moving around the room, touching things while she talked to Paul. He tensed a little and his eyes kept watching her hands as if he didn't like her handling his things.

Kim had a little smile on her face as she picked the shiny objects up and put them down. It was like she knew what Paul was feeling and was doing it on purpose.

That reminded me of times I played with Sharpfang's tail, even though I knew he hated it. I would keep it up while he flicked faster and faster and finally whipped around and snapped at me. It was the funniest thing.

Grinning now, I pulled myself up a little farther so I could see better.

She tossed the hair back from her face. Before I could duck she was staring right at me.

Her eyes widened.

I smiled to show how friendly I was.

Her hands flew up.

She stumbled backward and screamed in terror.

Chapter 28

Startled, I lost my hold. My claws scraped at the wall but couldn't grip. I scrabbled at air all the way down.

With that bloodcurling scream echoing in my ears, I hardly felt it when I hit the ground, twisting my leg under me.

The yapping and barking started in a frenzy. It seemed every animal for miles around was howling for my blood.

I lurched to my feet. Limping, I fled into the woods.

The pain in my leg hardly slowed me down at all. I ran like the wind. I ran faster than any of those puny Legwalkers' animals could go. But it didn't make me feel any better.

I ran until I couldn't hear the barking and yowling anymore. But I would always hear that scream. It echoed over and over in my brain. That terrified face was burned into my eyes forever.

What had I been thinking? As if a pretty Legwalker like that would ever be friends with me! I was a monster. The face I'd seen reflected in the dark window was real . . . and it was my face.

81

No wonder she had screamed in horror.

I would, too, if I could scream. But all I could do was howl. "Arooooooooh!" I threw back my head and felt the moonlight seek me out. I let out a long, mournful howl that froze the hearts of creatures for miles around.

I was back in the dark swamp where I belonged. My nostrils filled with the smell of mud and scummy water and rotting things. I would never get to be inside that warm, light-filled room.

Head hanging, I wandered through the swamp. I didn't want to run anymore. Running only reminded me of what I was.

But how had I become a monster? Why?

It must be the reason I was left here in the swamp so long ago. But why had I never changed before? What had I done to make this happen now?

I pushed on deeper into the swamp. What would happen to me? I wished I could sit down and cry, but the monster had no tears.

Walking slowly, not paying attention, I forgot all about the night creatures.

That was a big mistake.

I felt a hot breath on my shoulder.

It stank of evil.

Instantly, every nerve came alive. I leaped into the air just as a razor-sharp claw raked my shoulder.

My shoulder burned. In midair I twisted, kicking out with my long, clawed feet.

"Ooomph!" I heard as I bolted out of there.

Behind me the creature spat and cursed. *"I almost had him!"* it fumed. *"I was this close."*

I ran to a small muddy pool and plunged in. It smelled of snakes and slime. The scratch on my shoulder hissed and bubbled with steam. Shivering, I crouched until the icy water was up to my neck.

The werewolf called Ripper wasn't far behind.

"Oh, little one," he crooned in a false-friendly howl. *"Come out wherever you are, little Grrufff! You can't hide what you are, not from us you can't."*

It came nearer and I sank deeper, until only my nose poked out of the murky water.

The werewolf eyes glowed red in the darkness. It bent down and spoke close to the surface of the water, right beside my ear.

"We won't let you go this time, little one. You are one of us now!"

Chapter 29

The night creature called Ripper circled the pool, stalking me. It whispered and chuckled but in the end stamped its foot in frustration. It couldn't find me.

Other werewolves joined him. They flitted down from the trees like bats or appeared out of the shadows like nightmares.

But this was no dream.

"Have you got him?" they hissed among themselves. *"Is he here?"*

"No, I didn't get him," growled Ripper, grinding and gnashing his fangs. *"He must have slipped into one of these scummy puddles. I can't smell him anywhere, can you?"*

I heard a night creature shudder. *"Why would he want to do that? It's so cold and — and — wet!"*

"I say we forget about him," snapped another creature. *"We've got plenty of time to take care of that little fool. Right now my hunger is gnawing strong. We need to hunt!"*

There was a lot of growling and hissing of approval. But still the werewolves didn't move away.

"Let's go to the new town," one of them

snarled, smacking its lips, which were already crusted with rabbit blood. *"Lots of humans to choose from there."*

"This time let's take a child!" another suggested. Its eyes glowed like burning blood. *"They'll never know who did it. Wouldn't believe it if they saw us."* The creature cackled wildly. *"And we know who will get the blame, don't we?"*

Laughing and howling and slobbering, they started to move away, toward the place of lights. One paused and looked back over its shoulder, right into my eyes.

"Come along, Gruff!" it shrieked, showing sharp dripping fangs. *"You can have the first bite!"*

Chapter 30

As their cackling and snickering faded, I leaped from the small pool and followed. I couldn't let them harm the Legwalkers, especially the ones called Paul and Kim.

I ran, shuddering at the sound of their voices rummaging around inside my head. It was as if I were connected to them by an unbreakable thread. I could feel their evil thirst for blood.

There were so many of them and only one of me. If they got me, they'd make me a monster forever — but I had to follow. I had to stop them.

They drew closer to the town. I could sense them becoming more excited. They were biting each other and snarling as they fought over who would choose a victim.

Soon I was back in the place of twinkling lights, among the rows of Legwalker dens.

Ahead of me were the monsters.

Werewolves, their fangs dripping with anticipation, looked in through an open window at a small, sleeping Legwalker cub.

"That's the one," they hissed. *"Get it!"*

Suddenly one of them reached in with a long,

hairy arm and snatched up the tiny Legwalker.

Crouching by the side of the house, the were-wolf opened its great gaping jaws. Its yellow teeth glistened in the moonlight.

My stomach lurched and vomit rose into my throat. The little cub was doomed.

"Noooooooooo!" I screamed.

Chapter 31

I let out a great, furious howl and in one tremendous leap, cleared the whole pack of night creatures and thundered after the one with the cub.

My howl was fierce. It filled the night sky and put fear in the hearts of Legwalkers all over town. As I'd hoped, their sniffing animals set up a desperate clamor and soon the streets were filled with Legwalkers and barking, frenzied animals.

At the first bang of a Legwalker den opening, the werewolves behind me vanished. Somehow they just melted away into the darkness.

All except the one clutching the screaming cub. I was hot on its heels. But the blackness of the swamp was close. I knew that once the night creature reached the trees, I would never catch it. It was too skilled.

Putting on a burst of speed, I gained on the monster. My breath heaved hot in my lungs. I couldn't keep it up much longer. My throat burned and my legs ached with exhaustion.

The clamor of frenzied animals behind me grew louder. For the first time I felt a pang of fear as I pictured what would happen to me if they caught me.

A nasty thought popped into my mind. Hunger. I hadn't had anything to eat. Fresh meat, just a little, would make me stronger. Strong enough to escape the Legwalkers' animals.

I spat the thought from my mind. It was an alien, creeping, filthy thing put there by the desperate night creature I was chasing.

As I ran harder, I heard it snarl in fury. The trees loomed closer.

The werewolf lunged into the swamp. In my head I heard its silent howl of triumph.

I'd never find it now.

The Legwalker cub's cries weakened.

Chapter 32

The cub's cries! I felt a new surge of energy as I followed that faint trail of sound.

Breath rasping in my throat, I caught a glimpse of the werewolf as a beam of moonlight glinted on its scraggly fur. Taking a deep breath, I leaped into the air, aiming to come down on its back.

I missed. But not by much. Desperately I swiped at it and my claws raked the length of its back. The night creature screamed in fury and turned to face me, its long teeth bared in a snarl.

As it lunged at me, I sank my teeth into the arm that was holding the cub. With a hideous howl, the night creature dropped the cub. The werewolf's eyes burned with mindless vengeance as it turned to face me.

I felt its thoughts. First it would tear out my throat, then it would feast alone on the cub.

As it faced me it seemed to swell. I hadn't realized how much bigger than me it was. And I had been running so long. I was so tired.

"Now you die!" it screamed.

The creature reached for me with claws extended. As its claws sank into my shoulder I lowered my head and butted it as hard as I could in the stomach. Flesh tore from my shoulder as it fell.

Instantly it sprang to its feet, eyes blazing. A snarl started deep in its throat as it crouched to spring.

Then, without warning, it turned and disappeared into the swamp.

For a moment I just stood there, panting and bewildered. I hadn't butted it that hard. It could have torn me apart in a second. Then why didn't it?

Suddenly I jumped to my feet. The Legwalkers' animals! They were almost upon me. That was why the werewolf had run off.

Quickly I leaped into a tree. But then I became aware of the Legwalker cub crying nearby. It was half covered with dead leaves. I glanced toward the pack of crazed animals. They were already in among the trees.

Fixed as they were on hunting me, they might not see the Legwalker cub.

Gritting my teeth in fear, I dropped back to the ground. One of the animals caught my scent and started barking with excitement. I snatched up the Legwalker cub as the dog leaped for me.

Its jaws snapped on air as I sprang back into

the tree. The other Legwalker dogs gathered in a snarling pack below, throwing themselves uselessly into the air.

What could I do? I couldn't take the cub with me and I couldn't stay where I was. Legwalker voices grew louder every second I waited, agonizing. Finally I laid the cub down in a forked branch and swung into another tree.

"There's the baby!" a Legwalker cried. "It's alive!"

While the Legwalkers were busy rescuing their cub, I swung into another tree and then, dropping to the ground, easily outdistanced them.

I ran until I could no longer hear the Legwalkers or their frenzied animals. When I reached my old pool I slipped in, and for once the cold water felt good. The water hissed into steam as it touched the heat of my body.

Sinking slowly, I felt like I was lowering myself right into the swamp. I was a part of the swamp and it felt good. Creeping among the cypress roots, I let the cold water ease the tension from my muscles.

Soon it would be dawn and I would be myself again.

But one thought kept repeating in my mind. Sneering, one of the night creatures had said, just before they set off for the town, *"You know who will get the blame."*

Who did they mean? Me?

I told myself it didn't matter what they meant. In the morning I wouldn't be a monster anymore. The Legwalkers would never find me.

At last I fell asleep.

Chapter 33

I woke to the sweetest sound — Wolfmother howling for me, her lost cub.

The moon had set. It was just before dawn. I ached, and the nightmare of being a monster forever stuck to me like a bitter taste in the mouth.

The water was too dark to see through and my skin was too numb to feel. Was I still a monster?

My heart in my throat, I hauled myself out of the frigid water. And collapsed in relief. I had made it through the three nights of the wereing and I was Gruff again.

After a few minutes I was shivering so hard, I thought my bones would break. But I didn't care. It was all over now.

"Aroo-oo-ooh!"

I howled for joy and to let Wolfmother know I'd be along soon and then started scrounging for something to eat.

I was starved. But I barely had time to dig up a few roots and settle down with a twig next to a busy ant hole when I heard Wolfmother bounding toward me, giving soft calls.

I called back and stuffed a couple more fingerfuls of crunchy ants into my mouth before I set off to meet her.

Wolfmother found me in a clearing and licked my face in joy. I could tell she'd been frantic, worried that I'd never return.

"I'm okay!" I growled, nuzzling her warm fur. "I'm little Gruff again. Let's go home!"

With Wolfmother leading, the trip back to the den was quick. Wolfmother went on ahead, her tail wagging in anticipation of having all her family together again.

I had just started after her, when a sharp *CRACK!* stopped me in my tracks.

The noise exploded in my brain.

I had never heard such a thing before, but I knew instantly it was dangerous. Nothing ordinary could make such a shattering noise.

CRACK!

Deafened for an instant, I stood paralyzed with fear.

I knew in my bones that the noise meant death was coming — for someone.

Chapter 34

I was running for the safety of the wolf den when suddenly — *CRACK!* — leaves exploded off a tree above me. My head swam.

CRACK!

Animals fled in panic from the noise. As it died away the swamp was deathly quiet.

But into the silence came the excited shouts of Legwalkers.

Legwalkers!

I wanted to flee into the quiet of the deep swamp. But I couldn't run.

"There! I heard something over there!" a Legwalker yelled.

They must be hunting the hideous werewolves who prowled around their dens and peered in their windows and had stolen a cub. But I was safe. I looked like them now and not like the night creatures. Maybe the Legwalkers knew where to find the werewolves. If they did, I could help track them down.

Moving soundlessly, I slipped through the trees toward the Legwalkers. Something told me not to let them see me first, even though I was eager to help. Jumping over a narrow stream, I circled a boggy area, keeping to dry ground.

The Legwalkers didn't know the swamp very well and it was easy to creep up on them.

There were a bunch of them and they didn't look happy. These were big Legwalkers with harsh voices. They were mud-spattered and scratched up. One of them had a sniffing animal with him. The animal was tied to the Legwalker and was straining to pull the Legwalker along faster.

Each of the Legwalkers carried a long, stick-like thing. But it was no stick that ever came off a tree, I could see that.

A hidden squirrel chittered angrily from a branch just above me.

"Over there, Roy!"

Startled, one of the Legwalkers swung his stick toward the noise.

BOOM!

I dropped flat to the ground and covered my throbbing ears. Pieces of leaves rained down on me.

I raised my head an inch. The one with the dog turned on the one who'd used his stick.

"No more shooting, Roy," said another Leg-walker. "Not until we can see what we're shooting at. Now put your gun down," he said, scowling angrily.

Gun. I sounded the word in my head. Such a short word for such a big, nasty weapon.

The other one scowled, too, but lowered his gun. "Okay, but I hope you don't let those mangy wolves get away, Mike!"

Wolves! I understood that. And I heard the murderous threat in their voices.

My heart turned to stone. I felt like something heavy had wrapped itself around my neck and squeezed. How could they mistake the ghastly night creatures for wolves, beautiful wolves?

Maybe it was because I was the one they'd seen. I knew I was right when I told myself I was no hideous monster. I must have looked like a wolf to the Legwalkers.

My first instinct was to rush out and tell these Legwalkers what a big mistake they'd made. I was the one they wanted! They had to leave my family alone!

But I didn't know how to make the sounds they did. Even though I could understand a lot of it, I had no idea how they did it.

But I had to try. I had to make them believe me.

I took a deep breath and pushed aside the branch that hid me.

All I saw was a blur as Roy raised his gun.

CRACK!

Chapter 35

I fell flat to the ground, my face in the dirt.

"Dang it, Roy, you got to stop that," shouted Mike, the man with the sniffing dog. The animal was barking wildly.

Was I hit? My knee was throbbing. I didn't dare move. Somehow the Legwalkers hadn't seen me yet.

Mike took a step toward Roy. "I know little Benjy is your nephew and you're upset," he said, "but we all love the boy, too, and we want to make sure nothing like that happens again."

Benjy? That must be the cub's name. Was it all right? I tensed, waiting to hear.

"Wolves are smart animals," said Mike through clenched teeth. "And a wolf that can sneak up and snatch a two-year-old child from his crib like that is vicious. If it weren't for the dogs we might have lost Benjy. Benjy was lucky, but the next child might not be. No more shooting at trees, Roy. Save your bullets for the wolves. I want to get those wolves."

I remembered the night creatures cackling when they said they knew who'd be blamed. I'd thought they meant me, but it was my wolf family that was being blamed, just as the night creatures planned all along!

"Burn down this whole miserable swamp!" Roy burst out. "That's what I said we ought to do last night and that's what I still say. Who needs it!"

"That wouldn't get the wolves," Mike insisted. "They'd only run off. Like they're going to do if you keep shooting that gun. Follow my plan and I promise you that we'll get those wolves."

His eyes narrowed to mean slits and he smacked his animal — who was straining in my direction — to quiet him.

I wriggled back into the underbrush, getting myself hidden again. They would never listen to me. They had revenge in mind and couldn't think of anything else.

My only chance was to hear their plan and find a way to stop them.

"The wolves haven't been hunted around here," said Mike. "They won't be expecting us to come after them. They'll think we're after deer. I'll bet they're holed up in their den right this minute, sleeping off a long night's mischief and waiting for us to go away."

"You think so?"

"Sure. They know we could never find their den on our own. But what they haven't reckoned on is Lady." Mike leaned down and patted the panting dog. "Lady can track a wolf like nobody's business. She'll lead us straight to their den."

Mike looked around at the other Legwalkers, his eyes cold. "That's when we use our guns. They'll be like sitting ducks. We'll kill every one of the beasts, down to the last mewling cub."

Chapter 36

"Yeah, come on, boys, let's get 'em!"

"We'll shoot those wolves to pieces!"

"They'll wish they never heard of Fox Hollow!"

"Think they can attack our kids — we'll show 'em!"

Killing words ringing in my ears. I fled back through the swamp, running for the den as fast as I could go.

My legs seemed to get tangled up in every root, tripped by every mud hole. I could hear the Legwalkers behind me. They were slow, but the sniffing dog was leading them straight for the den.

My breath whistled in my lungs. I ran faster.

Finally the clearing was in sight. I crouched in the bushes outside the clearing and looked back.

The Legwalkers were stumbling through the underbrush, grunting with effort and annoyance. They were close but they weren't in sight yet.

I dashed across the clearing and dove into the den.

They were all there, huddled deep inside.

The wolf family that had raised me, protected me, given me a home when no one wanted me. I was gasping for breath so hard I couldn't make a sound. Wolfmother made a welcoming noise in her throat and put a reassuring paw on my head. Sharpfang made room for me to squeeze in beside him.

They thought the hunters had frightened me! I barked, shaking my head vigorously, trying to warn them of the danger. But wolves didn't have the sounds for everything I needed to explain. I barked for danger and flight and ran at the entrance again and again until Thornclaw began to get annoyed.

The rest of them looked at me with sad, uncomprehending eyes. All they saw was poor dumb Gruff who didn't know when to stay silent and lay low.

Time was running out.

The Legwalker hunters were getting closer and closer.

"Grrraaaw," I growled harder, making the sounds for terrible danger.

Wolfmother put her paw on my head again, pressing down like she did when she wanted the cubs to lie still.

I was frantic. In minutes the Legwalkers

would be here with their guns and the wolves would be trapped.

I pointed over my shoulder. "Woof," I said, trying to imitate the dog. "Woof."

Sharpfang bared his teeth to me, a warning to be silent.

There was only one thing left to do. The Legwalkers were almost at the clearing.

I grabbed the cubs and snatched them out from behind Wolfmother. I lunged for the opening of the den. Now Wolfmother would have to follow.

But Thornclaw leaped across the floor. Before I could push the cubs out, he silently grasped my neck in his mouth.

This was going to hurt, I thought, closing my eyes. He might even rip my throat out, though he wouldn't mean to, of course.

But there was no more time to reason with them. I braced myself.

Chapter 37

"YELP!"

That wasn't me!

The wolves jumped to attention, ears quivering.

Thornclaw let go of my neck. The cubs squirmed free and scrambled behind Wolf-mother.

"Hang it, Roy, you stepped right on Lady's tail," I heard Mike say furiously, only yards away. "That's torn it for sure. Now they know we're here."

"I say we rush 'em now, guns blazing," said a third voice.

"Yeah!"

A gray blur swept past me. Sharpfang burst out of the den, growling ferociously.

CRACK!

"There he goes! Get him!"

Sharpfang bounded across the clearing and disappeared into the swamp.

Thornclaw dashed to the door of the den. He stood there, growling and showing his teeth, making himself a target.

CRACK!

Thornclaw sprang for the trees, heading in

the opposite direction Sharpfang had taken.

"I see him!"

The Legwalkers split up, going after Sharpfang and Thornclaw into the swamp.

I looked over my shoulder into the depths of the den. Wolfmother was trying to drag Leaper and Snapjaw out, but the cubs were terrified and struggling. All their lives they'd been taught that the den was the world's one safe place. And now when real danger came for the first time, Wolfmother was trying to make them leave. They scrabbled at the wall as if they could hide inside it.

I reached out, grabbed the cubs, and hauled them after me, scrambling for the opening of the den.

Footsteps pounded the ground close by. "Keep going," shouted a voice. "I'll shoot the ones trapped in the den."

I clutched the cubs to me. But I was too slow. The Legwalkers would catch me for sure.

There was only one thing I could do.

Wolfmother nudged my arm and I put the cubs down. She grasped Leaper in her teeth, holding her by the scruff of the neck.

My stomach flip-flopped. Wolfmother could only take one cub at a time.

Maybe once she'd gotten away, I could come

back for Snapjaw. I swallowed hard and tried not to think.

Frantically I started scooping up pebbles. Outside, I could hear the Legwalker creeping through the bushes, thinking he was being sneaky and quiet.

It had to be now, ready or not.

I sprang out of the den opening and threw a pebble over the Legwalker's head. It landed behind him, rustling up some leaves. As I'd hoped, he whirled and fired his gun.

CRACK!

My ears ringing, I fired off another small rock. This one hit him in the head.

But before he could turn again, I was up the tree that grew outside the den. I began pelting the Legwalker with rocks.

He fell to his knees.

"RRRuuff," I barked. "RRRRRuuff." That told Wolfmother to flee, now, fast.

All that practicing with my throwing stick was proving good for something. I never missed.

"Ow!" squeaked the Legwalker. "Hey! Ouch!"

I grinned to myself as I glimpsed Wolfmother slink out of the den and slip soundlessly into the woods.

The Legwalker couldn't get up. He couldn't even see what was hitting him. Now if I could only keep him down until Wolfmother could get back for Snapjaw.

But it wasn't to be.

CRACK! CRACK!

I heard the whine of the gun-arrow as it whistled past my ear.

SMACK!

Another one smashed into the tree trunk I was balanced against. It had missed me by a hair. The things that came out of the guns were tinier than my pebbles. But a lot more dangerous. *CRACK!* Another one hit the tree and buried itself instantly.

The other Legwalkers had come back.

"Kill it!" they all shouted.

It. They meant me.

Chapter 38

I couldn't let them get me here. Snapjaw was still inside the den!

The poor cub must be frightened to death.

I took my biggest rock and heaved it into a tree over the Legwalkers' heads, outside the clearing. It made a big, satisfying noise in the leaves.

"Whoa, where is it?" cried one of the Legwalkers.

"Wolves don't climb trees," yelled another.

"Just shoot it — we'll figure it out later."

Gunfire erupted, ripping leaves and sending squawking birds in every direction.

The trees here were close together and I was able to swing myself into first one, then another, moving farther away from the den. There was so much commotion, none of the Legwalkers noticed.

Then I saw a sight that made my heart leap with joy.

Sharpfang! He dashed out of the woods, streaking for the den. He dove inside, and when he emerged he had Snapjaw between his teeth.

I howled and growled, raining rocks down on the Legwalkers to distract them, and when

I looked back, Sharpfang was gone.

And I was out of pebbles.

I hunched in my tree as bullets whizzed over my head, feeling very much alone.

Then I started to wonder — could I go after my wolf family? Not now, but maybe after dark when the Legwalkers had given up and gone back to their dens.

I needed my family. I ached for them. Where would I be without Wolfmother and Thornclaw and Sharpfang and Snapjaw and Leaper?

But then, as the Legwalkers crashed around below me, I realized it could never be. The Legwalkers wouldn't give up so easily and my family needed to be on the run. I was too slow. I'd just hold them back.

The only way my wolf family could survive was without me.

CRACK! I ducked as a bullet ripped through the leaves over my head. One thing I had to do, I had to get out of this tree. But with no pebbles left, how could I distract the Legwalkers long enough?

Then off in the distance, I heard Sharpfang howl. Howl as if he wanted to be heard. As if he wanted the hunters to know where he was. What was going on?

"Over there!" Roy shouted. "Get it!"

It was getting the Legwalkers all excited, that was for sure. They crashed off in that direction as fast as they could go. I almost laughed, easing myself down from the tree.

By the time the Legwalkers got there, Sharpfang would be miles away.

Down on the ground, I sighed. Which way should I go? What did it matter? I was part Legwalker, part monster, and deep inside I was part wolf, too. But nobody wanted me.

I stiffened at a small sound in the bushes nearby. Again my pulse began to race.

Chapter 39

It was Wolfmother.

Cautiously, the wolf crept out from the underbrush. She held Leaper in her mouth.

I whined in surprise and fear and barked to send her away. The hunters could be back any minute.

Wolfmother growled softly in her throat and crouched on the ground, folding all four legs. It was what she used to do when I was little. I would climb on her back and ride like the wind.

But now I was too big.

She growled again and fixed me with an impatient eye. Maybe it would work. I longed for it to work.

Biting my lip I straddled her back. Wolfmother stood and I held on, shakily. She took a step, then another.

But suddenly the Legwalker's dog, Lady, began to bark in the distance. It was a strangled yelp, like she was struggling with all her might against the tie that held her back.

I knew what had happened. The dog had scented Wolfmother. Wolfmother knew it, too. She began to run. But with me on her back she was slow and her feet sank too deeply into the soft ground.

Excited, the Legwalkers freed the dog to give chase. The yelping of the dog and the harsh shouts of the Legwalkers chilled my blood. They were coming our way, fast.

Already Wolfmother was tiring.

I loved Wolfmother more than life itself, so I did the only thing I could. I let go. Rolling onto the ground, I urged her to run without me, to leave me behind. She whined and tossed her head, rolling her eyes. I barked roughly, begging her to run.

Leaper gave a pained little cry and that decided it. Wolfmother gave me one last, mournful look and then disappeared into the swamp with a flash of her bushy tail.

I brushed the tears from my eyes, filled my fists with rocks again, and scrambled into the nearest tree.

Soon the hunters came tramping back, complaining because they hadn't killed any wolves. I was so mad and upset that I didn't care if they saw me. I reared back and threw as hard as I could. *POW!* The rock hit Roy right in the nose.

"Look, up in the tree!"

CRACK! CRACK! The bullets came whizzing by. If I stayed in the tree they'd get me for sure.

So I leaped down to the ground, ready to run for my life.

"Look!" somebody cried. "Is that thing human?"

I turned, but the hunters blocked my way. They were going to kill me, no doubt about it. But if I had to die I was going to die like a wolf, brave and true.

I dropped down on all fours and gave my attack howl. "AROOOOOOH!" Then I ran right at them, snapping and snarling, feeling the wildness in my heart.

They had me in their sights now. They couldn't miss. It was all over.

I threw back my head and let out a long "farewell" howl to my family.

The Legwalker called Mike was staring at me. His eyes were terrible. Slowly he brought up his rifle.

Chapter 40

I was about to die, and I felt so lonesome and miserable I didn't even care.

Mike's finger squeezed on the trigger.

"No!" Roy shouted grabbing Mike's rifle. "Are you guys blind? That's not a wolf, that's a boy!"

"He ain't like no boy I've ever seen. He's a wild thing."

Mike and Roy started arguing. Paying attention to each other and not to me. Now was my chance to get away.

I started backing up slowly, not making a sound. Let these stupid Legwalkers argue all they wanted. Meanwhile I'd escape. It didn't matter that I had nowhere to go, no place to call home. At least I'd be free. Until the next full moon.

I was backing up slowly when something hard and heavy hit me from behind.

The world went black.

Chapter 41

Bouncing.

I was bouncing. Wrapped tight in something scratchy and musty smelling that had last been used by mice — and not recently, either. I didn't know if I could move.

Where was I?

Carefully, I opened one eye and took a quick peep. Legwalkers! All around me!

I was their prisoner.

Two of them were carrying me, having made a sling out of an old blanket. What were they going to do to me? I had to try to get away.

Desperately, I watched for my chance. But the Legwalkers on either side of me stayed close, hemming me in.

All of a sudden the tension seemed to whoosh right out of the Legwalkers. They all began to breathe easier and walked with more confidence. I noticed the trees begin to thin out. The sunshine was brighter.

We were getting close to the place of the Legwalker dens.

Then one of the Legwalkers let out a shout and raised his arm. I heard answering shouts coming from nearby.

My insides trembled with fear.

"We bagged ourselves a wolf-boy!" shouted Mike. He laughed, but not like he thought it was funny. More like he was nervous.

I heard footsteps come running to meet us. At the edge of the woods the Legwalkers put me down. They all took a step back and looked at me. The whole town seemed to be crowding around, staring at me.

"Mike nearly shot the kid," said the one called Roy.

"I did not. I always shoot what I aim at, unlike some I know. The wolf-boy just had the wind knocked out of him. Watch out, he bites."

"Was he really living in the woods?" said a new voice, pushing through the crowd to stand beside me. It was Paul, the young Legwalker whose den I'd spied on.

"He was helping the wolves," said one of the hunters in a grim voice. "Kept us from hitting any of them. Fixed it so they got clean away."

"He must have been raised by them wolves," said the one called Mike. "Knew all their calls and everything."

"Cool!" said Paul, his eyes shining. "Hey, Dad, he doesn't have any place to live now. Could he come home with us?"

"With us?" One of the hunters scratched his head. "We'll have to call Social Services. But I suppose he can come with us until the authorities figure out what to do with him."

"I'd be careful," said Mike warningly. "That boy's more beast than human."

I turned my head a little to look at Paul.

"He moved," cried a new voice, a young voice.

It was the Legwalker I'd frightened, the female from Paul's room. Kim. She ran forward and dropped to her knees beside me.

I tensed with fear. Did she recognize me from the full-moon night? Did she know I was the monster who'd made her scream?

"This is so cool," said Paul, his eyes shining. "A real live wolf-boy!"

Kim put her hand on my forehead. It felt warm and soft, like the first real touch of summer sun. "Can you speak?" she asked me, looking straight into my eyes.

"He sure can howl," laughed one of the hunters. Another one tried to imitate me, sounding more like a sick pig than a wolf.

"Better not get so close, Kim," said her father. "He might bite. I imagine he's pretty frightened."

"Stop!" cried Kim, looking distressed. "He understands you. You do understand, don't you?"

I swallowed. My heart thumped. If I could make Legwalker sounds, then maybe they wouldn't hurt me.

"Y-yes," I said. It came out of my throat sounding like a wolf growl and a snake's hiss all mixed up together. The hunters scowled. One of them fingered the trigger on his gun. Even Kim looked baffled and a little frightened.

They couldn't understand me. My throat felt dry and my tongue was too thick. But I had to try again.

"Y-yes," I said. "Yes."

Chapter 42

Kim's eyes widened.

Suddenly Paul jumped up. "Mom," he shouted, running toward a pretty Legwalker with short brown hair who was threading her way through the crowd. "They found a wolf-boy. Can he stay with us, please?"

The female he called "Mom" had a round, friendly face. The way she looked at me reminded me strangely of Wolfmother. She stared at me for a while, then nodded and said, "We can take him home while we make some calls, see who's responsible for him."

"Not so fast, Mrs. Parker," said the hunter called Mike. "This wild boy can wait in the town jail. He's the one fixed it so all those killer wolves got away. Maybe they'll be back for him — and we'll be waiting."

"N-no," I cried, jumping up. Mike raised his rifle. One of the other hunters put a hand on Mike's arm, pushing the rifle away, but he was frowning suspiciously at me.

I wanted to tell them they were blaming the wrong ones. "It's the night creatures," I wanted to say. "The wolves wouldn't hurt anybody."

But I didn't know the words. All I could do was shake my head wildly.

Another hunter spoke up. "It's on account of him the beasts came to town in the first place. Living with a human boy, they lost all their natural fear of people. I agree with Mike."

"No," I said, struggling to get my awkward tongue around the sounds. "N-not wolves! N-not wolves!"

Another Legwalker stepped out of the crowd, holding the little Legwalker cub I'd saved from the night creatures. "Not wolves, eh? Tell that to my son, Benjy," he said, staring at me stonily. "He was dragged right out of his crib last night." He jutted his chin at me, looking like he wouldn't mind dragging me off somewhere. "Right through an open window."

Little Benjy looked at me with wide blue eyes. He clutched his bandaged arm to his side as if he was afraid I might sink my teeth into it.

"If our dogs hadn't gone tearing after them, they'd have dragged Benjy right into the woods," the Legwalker continued. "I got a pretty good look at them and they sure looked like wolves to me."

All around him Legwalkers grumbled in agreement, nodding their heads and glaring at me.

My head was a jumble. I needed to warn them of the real danger — the night creatures — but without Legwalker sounds, I couldn't do anything but shake my head and make a weird moaning sound.

"I think he's trying to tell us it was some other creature that came after Benjy," said Kim suddenly. "I told you I saw something really weird outside Paul's window, right, Mom? Something horrible and monstrous. Definitely not a wolf."

"Now, Kim," said the Mother Legwalker in a warning voice. "I thought we agreed it was a raccoon you saw."

"No way," muttered Kim, so quietly that no one heard her but me.

"Yeah," said Roy. He laughed and slapped his leg. "Maybe we got monsters in Fox Hollow. Big monster raccoons with glowing eyes. That what you're trying to tell us, wolf-boy?"

Startled, I wheeled around to stare at him.

Roy grinned at me but there was nothing friendly about it. "Don't look at me, kid. I'm not the one's been seeing things. In fact, you're the strangest thing I've seen in a long time."

Kim's mother clapped a hand on my shoulder. "I've heard enough of this," she said. "I won't have you badgering a young boy. He

123

looks like he's been through plenty already. He's coming home with us and that's the end of it. Come along, Paul, Kim."

They helped me get to my feet and led me away. I could have run, but something inside me wanted to stay.

"I'd keep an eye out tonight if I were you, Mrs. Parker," said Mike in a mean voice. "Those killers will be back. Might be they'll come looking for their human mascot. You better hope he doesn't help them get their big teeth into Paul or Kim."

The one called Mom looked at me with concern and then shook her head, as if she didn't want to believe anything so evil.

Paul and Kim led me through the crowd. People stared at me curiously. Some backed away as if they thought I might bite them.

I missed my wolf family terribly and I had a feeling it wasn't going to be easy becoming a Legwalker.

Kim touched my shoulder.

"Do you have a name?" she asked. "Can you tell me what it is?"

So I told her. And wished I hadn't.

Chapter 43

"Grrrrruff!" said Paul up close to my ear. Then he fell back, doubled over his stomach, laughing. Kim was biting her lip, trying not to laugh, too.

"Stop it!" said Mrs. Parker sharply. "You know better than to be making fun of people, Paul."

We were walking down a wide path with big blocky structures on both sides. New words swirled around in my head.

People. Boy. Girl. It seemed the Legwalkers had lots of names for themselves and they all meant something a little different. Like "Mom" and "Mrs. Parker," two names for the same Mother Legwalker.

"This is our house," said Paul, stopping in front of the den I'd prowled around last night.

"First thing, we've got to get you cleaned up," said Mrs. Parker. She fitted a small metal thing into a tiny hole and a piece of the wall swayed open.

The inside was not dark because of the squares — windows — which let in light. But it was full of strange, frightening objects. I stayed close to the entrance, ready to make my escape.

"Come in and sit down, Gruff," said Mrs. Parker, heading deeper into the den. "Paul, shut the door."

Paul nudged me inside and swung the entranceway closed behind me. It shut with a quiet click that echoed as loud in my head as the nasty crack of shooting guns. I tensed.

I was alone in a strange den with strange creatures who looked like me but whose friends had just tried to kill my family.

All of a sudden I couldn't breathe. Air stuck in my throat like a splinter of pigeon bone. The den was large but the walls seemed to move closer when I wasn't looking. And now there was no way out!

"Are you all right, Gruff?" asked Kim, cocking her head and looking sharply at me. "Sit down, I'll get you some juice."

Sit down. That's what Mrs. Parker had told me to do when we first came in. Maybe that's what you were supposed to do when you entered a Legwalker den.

I folded my legs under me and sank to the floor, every muscle stiff with dread. Sitting like this I couldn't run or leap. I was completely at their mercy.

My heart began to hammer as I noticed both

Paul and Kim staring at me with peculiar expressions. Then they looked at each other and broke out laughing.

I jumped up, ready to bolt for the door even though I had no place to go. But Kim put her hand on my arm. "I'm sorry, Gruff," she said. "We didn't mean to laugh at you. We were laughing at ourselves, really. Because we didn't have sense enough to tell you about chairs."

Although I couldn't understand all the words, I heard the friendliness in her voice. She was sorry she had frightened me. Paul nodded and tried hard not to laugh anymore, though he couldn't stop the corners of his mouth from twitching.

"In a house," said Kim, gesturing at the walls around her, "you sit in a chair. Like this." She walked over to one of the den's strange bulky objects, turned around, and sat in it just like I might sit on a rock.

There she got up and gestured at me to try it. It was like sitting on a cloud. I sank into the soft seat and the padded back seemed to sigh as I leaned into it.

"I'm glad to see you've made Gruff comfortable," said Mrs. Parker, reappearing. I looked at her quickly, tensing up again. She smiled at me but there was a strain around her eyes, almost like pain. Her eyes fluttered over my torn deerskins and bare feet.

"Paul, I think you should take Gruff upstairs and run him a bath," she said. "You're both about the same size. He can wear some of your clothes. Meanwhile I'll make some calls and we'll figure out what to do with him."

"Come on, Gruff," said Paul, jumping up.

They had a clever arrangement for getting to the top of the house — *stairs*, Paul called it.

"This is my room," he said, pausing before a closed door.

It felt strange to be standing here, already knowing what I would see. I felt guilty about that but proud, too. It was all mixed up.

"You're going to love this," he said, flashing me a grin.

He threw open the door and there were all his shiny things.

I hesitated, suddenly nervous again. Just last night I'd been thinking we might be friends, and then Kim had screamed and I'd known I was just a monster. Now, here I was, inside their den. It felt wrong somehow.

But Paul misunderstood my awkwardness. "I knew you'd be impressed," he said. "Pretty great, isn't it?"

I remembered a word he'd used when the hunters first brought me out of the swamp. "Coo-ul," I said. It came out sounding a little like a wolf's bark, but Paul was delighted. He clapped me on the back and whooped.

Then he led me around the room, showing me his stuff, rattling off names that meant nothing to me — *Mars probe, space shuttle, Wright brothers' plane, Sherman tank* — after a while I stopped listening, though I loved looking. I wanted to touch, too, but they looked so delicate I thought my clumsy fingers might crush them.

Still, I wasn't really impressed until Paul showed me a table covered with tiny pieces. "This is what I'm working on now," he said, pointing to a colorful picture on a box. "It's a space station."

Only then did it dawn on me that he had actually built all these things. I looked around again, in awe.

"Maybe we can work on them together," said Paul. "I can read you the instructions. Once you learn a little more English."

Paul's mother called from downstairs. "Paul, how are you coming along up there? I don't hear any water running."

"Okay, Mom!" yelled Paul. He shrugged his

shoulders at me. "Bath time. Come on."

We went down the hall to a small room filled with more strange objects, but different from the objects called furniture. Everything was shiny and hard.

"This is the bathtub." Paul bent over and water suddenly began gushing out of the wall.

I jumped back in fear, but he didn't seem alarmed.

"Here's the soap," he said, "and towels are in here. I'll get you a pair of my jeans and a T-shirt."

He left me there. Steam rose from the rushing water. Soon the big tub would overflow, like some of our swamp ponds did in the spring. But in the swamp the water just ran over the ground. Here there was no ground. I stared in dread, not knowing what to do to stop it. The water rose higher.

It began to lap at the edge of the tub. A dribble ran over. Then a stream.

"Yikes!" Paul dashed into the room and a second later there was quiet. He had stopped the water.

"I should have known," he said to himself. He turned to me. "You have to get in it," he said in a loud voice as if I was deaf. He no longer looked so friendly. He sniffed and wrin-

130

kled his nose. "You have to take a bath. In case you don't know it, you smell kind of swampy." I realized he was trying to say I stunk.

Of course I smell swampy, I wanted to tell him. I've been up to my neck in swamp water all night. A swim in the nice clean sun-warmed pond was what I needed.

Paul sighed. "Take off those animal skins," he said, acting out the words. He went behind me and shut the door while I stripped off my skins.

As soon as the door was closed the steam swarmed in on me, filling my nose and throat. I couldn't breathe.

"Good," said Paul. "Now get into the tub."

I stood there, panic rising in me. This was no sun-warmed pond. These Legwalkers didn't want to help me, they wanted to boil me! They wanted me dead!

"It's not that bad," said Paul. "I do it every day. Almost every day."

When I still didn't move, he frowned. I could see the menace in his face now. He was out to get me!

Paul grabbed my arm and started dragging me to the steaming water. Desperately I glanced at the window. It was closed and it was too small for me to fit through, anyway.

I had no choice.

I'd have to push Paul into the hot water. It would just be a quick push. I just needed to stop him long enough to run to his room and escape through his window.

I waited until we were right beside the tub. He gave me a push. I reached up and grabbed him by the back of the neck.

I was strong and he wasn't expecting it. I twisted my hip and threw him off balance.

"Whoa!" yelled Paul. But in a flash he had grabbed my long hair and yanked me after him.

Chapter 44

Aaah! I was scalded. Paul's hand thrashed up out of the water and — *WOMP!* — he pushed my head under.

I struggled up and grabbed hold of him to push him away. He slipped and went under the surface, dragging me with him. I heaved myself up and took a breath.

But Paul was making strange sputtering noises. Was he drowning? I tried to lift him, but my feet went out from under me. The tub was slippery. I reached for him again, but he twisted away.

Then, with a great splash, he burst out of the water.

"Wow," said Paul, still sputtering. "You're strong." He was laughing!

Then he lunged for me and we were both thrashing and splashing in the water and I was laughing, too. It was just like the times Sharpfang and I wrestled each other in the pond until we were both exhausted.

Finally Paul stood, shaking his head and sending drops of water flying everywhere. "Look at this mess," he said in an awed tone. "Mom's going to kill us."

Mom? Kill? I felt a leap of panic. Would the Mom Legwalker think I had tried to drown her cub? Was that why she would kill me?

But Paul didn't seem worried. He got some things he called *towels* and sopped up the puddles of water on the floor. "There," he said. "That ought to do it." His wet clothes stuck to him and I realized he was almost as thin as me.

"Well as long as I'm in here I might as well show you what to do," said Paul, who didn't sound worried anymore.

After he'd acted out the bath he showed me how to empty the tub and turn on the shower, which was like a rainstorm for one person. Actually, it wasn't until he showed me the shower that I really understood. Lots of times, in the summer at least, I'd use the rain to get clean.

Once I had the tub to myself, I discovered I kind of liked it. The water was warmer than any pond, almost the same temperature as my skin, and the sudsy soap felt slick and smelled nice.

Paul left me there, splashing in the tub, and the next thing I knew someone was pounding on the door.

"Gruff! You still in there?"

I'd fallen asleep!

It took me a minute to remember what Paul

had showed me about emptying the tub and turning on the shower. And it took me a lot longer to figure out how to put on the strange-feeling skins Paul called *clothes*.

When finally I came back into his room, Paul was looking at pictures of monsters, just like he had been last night.

"I was beginning to think you'd drowned," he said, tossing down the monster pictures.

Why was Paul so interested in monsters? Did he know about the werewolves? I picked up the thing with the pictures, made a puzzled face, and raised my eyebrows.

"That? That's a comic book," explained Paul. "Cool, isn't it? I've got lots more, but right now it's lunchtime and afterward Kim wants to give you an English lesson."

Lunch turned out to mean food.

"Ham sandwich and milk," said Kim.

I tried to eat it like she and Paul did, but around the meat there was all this doughy stuff that stuck to the roof of my mouth. When I took that off it was fine, although the meat didn't taste like any animal I was familiar with.

Afterward Kim and Paul spent the whole day pointing at things and saying the names and making me say them.

They laughed at my voice, which I didn't like

135

much, but Kim said they couldn't help it because I sounded like a rusty hinge. I didn't
know what that was and they couldn't show
me because, said Paul, Fox Hollow was a new
town and didn't have any rust yet.

"We've only lived here a month," said Kim.
"So we're getting used to things, too, just like
you."

Just like me. If only she knew what "just like
me" meant, she'd run screaming from the
room.

Chapter 45

Later we had something called *supper*.

Mrs. Parker had everybody sit down and then she put something called *plates* in front of us.

On the plates were steaming piles of long white worms covered in slimy blood. Was this what humans ate?

"Yum, spaghetti and meatballs," said Kim. "My favorite."

Kim showed me how to use a fork. I watched her and Paul and Mr. and Mrs. Parker twirl the things on their forks and chomp away with enthusiasm, as if worms were really their favorite food.

I was interested though I'd never seen such long worms. It took forever to wind the slippery things onto my fork thing. The worms kept falling off when I got them almost to my mouth. Kim almost choked laughing and bits of chewed white worm spilled down her chin.

Finally I managed to get some into my mouth. Mmm. Good. And they were easier to chew than most of the food I was used to.

I stuck my fork back in and once again the worms fell off. I could starve to death at this rate. Everyone else was half done. Soon they'd be sniffing at mine.

I took a bite of meatball. The taste exploded in my mouth. Meat, but not like real meat. It was all grainy bits stuck together, but it was delicious. I dove into the worms for another try.

"Maybe I ought to cut that spaghetti up for you, Gruff," said Mrs. Parker, taking my plate.

Kim giggled. I couldn't see what was funny, but it didn't matter because now I could fork up spaghetti by the mouthful. In a minute I was done. When I looked up, the whole family was staring at me.

I stiffened in fear. Could they see somehow that I wasn't like them? Could they see what I really was?

But they weren't staring like my wolf family had done the first night of the wereing. This was different. More a wondering, apart kind of staring.

"I've never seen anyone eat so fast," said Mrs. Parker with a small breathless laugh. "Would you like some more?"

I tensed up again. Was she offering me her own portion? Wolfmother hadn't done that since I was old enough to chew for myself. Did Mrs. Parker think I was a helpless baby?

"No, po-leese," I said, in my rusty-hinge voice. Mrs. Parker was always telling Paul and Kim to say "please" and "thank you" when they spoke to her.

Unlike the wolves, humans sat at the table and waited until everyone else was done eating. And nobody snatched anything from anyone else's plate. It was all so strange, so very strange.

With my belly full of worm-spaghetti, I suddenly felt so sleepy I could hardly hold my head up.

Finally Mrs. Parker pushed back her chair. "I've fixed up the guest room for you, Gruff. Paul, show him where it is and lend him some pajamas."

Pajamas? What was pajamas? Was pajamas going to be as scary as taking a bath?

Chapter 46

Pajamas turned out to be the softest, most colorful clothes I'd ever seen. "That's what we wear to bed," Paul explained.

I wondered why they didn't wear them all the time, they were so comfortable, but I wasn't yet sure enough of the words to ask. I liked the feel of these skins but I was worried about these humans. They were so used to warm water and soft clothes. Even with their wonderful weapons they were too trusting to save themselves from the werewolves. They didn't even realize they had taken a monster into their den.

"And just in case you haven't figured it out, this is a bed," Paul said. He bounced on the thing called a *bed*. "You sleep here, okay?"

I nodded. I knew what *sleep* was. I sighed, wondering where my wolf family was sleeping tonight.

"Another thing," Paul said. "See these little button things? These are light switches."

He clicked one on and the room went dark. I jumped, frightened. He clicked the switch again and the light came back on, just like magic.

"Turn that out when you're ready," he said. "Or I guess you can sleep with the lights on if you're scared."

"Not sk-eered," I said.

"Great," he said with a yawn. "See you in the morning."

He left, closing the door. I was alone. I shut off the lights — now the room was more like my old wolf den. The darkness was comforting, but I missed my family. Would I ever be a human? Would I ever see Wolfmother again?

I felt uneasy. Light drew me to the window.

The moon. It wasn't full now — it had no special power over me — but still it called to me.

I thought of my wolf family out there somewhere. Would they have found a new den yet? Probably not. Leaper and Snapjaw would be frightened. I wished I was there to help Wolfmother calm them.

But there was something about this human family that stirred deep feelings inside me, too. Even though I was always doing things a little wrong and making people laugh, I felt like I knew them.

Things were strange, but some things were familiar, too. Part of me that had been asleep for a long, long time was waking up. I was

141

afraid of the future but excited, too. Maybe I could belong here.

But my eye caught the moon again and my spirits fell. What would happen with the next full moon? I would become a monster again, that's what.

I'd have to leave this place and my new friends. I had to go back to the swamp and find a place to hide before the next full moon. I couldn't take a chance on letting a monster — me — loose in Fox Hollow.

I sighed and was starting to turn away from the window when a man came down the street. He turned off the road and headed toward the woods. Then he stopped.

He seemed to be waiting for something.

The hairs on the back of my neck bristled. There was something very strange about the way the man was acting.

I kept watching.

After a few minutes more men appeared in the street. They came from several directions. They joined the first man and together they started toward the woods. What were they doing out there?

They all stopped in a patch of silver moonlight.

One by one they threw their heads back and

opened their mouths. No sound came out—they were howling silently!

Somehow I knew what was going to happen next. And it did.

Suddenly their clothing burst at the seams and fell away from their bodies. They dropped to all fours, covered with wiry gray hair. Their bodies twisted and writhed in the moonlight as muscles rippled under flesh.

Night creatures. These weren't men, they were werewolves!

When the Change was complete the creatures crouched motionless for a second. Then, all together, they swung around. Red eyes like hot coals lifted to my window, fixed on my face. I couldn't move.

The hideous night creatures all began to laugh silently, showing yellow fangs. I heard their voices in my mind.

"There's no escape," they howled in my head. *"No escape for little Gruff. And no escape for Fox Hollow!"*

Don't Miss
THE WEREWOLF CHRONICLES
Book II: *Children of the Wolf*

Once the Change was complete, Ripper sucked in a huge lungful of air and rose up on his hind legs. The other werewolves gathered around him, cringing from the reach of his long curved claws. They waited for his command.

Ripper's burning eyes stared them down. When all the werewolves were still as death, Ripper opened his great jaw, showing rows of glistening razor-sharp teeth.

His words echoed inside my head.

"My brothers, the time is soon. On the first night of the full moon we will take the children of Fox Hollow. Our bite will free them. Their blood will be our blood. There can be no escape."

As these terrible words burned into my brain, a silent cheer went up from the listening werewolves and pounded in my head.

"We must be ready," thundered Ripper,

although the sleeping people of Fox Hollow would hear no sound. *Each of you knows what to do."*

"YESSSS!" screamed the werewolves inside my head. They began dancing with glee around their leader but stopped the instant he raised one claw-tipped hand.

"Go!" Ripper commanded. He took a step forward. The werewolves scattered out of his path, leaped into the air, and disappeared into the night.

The great werewolf Ripper stood motionless, the moon spilling cold light over his shaggy head and muscled shoulders.

I held my breath. What was he doing?

Ripper raised his head and shot one burning glance into my tree. I pressed myself against the rough bark, faint with terror. He knew I was here! He took a step toward the tree.

His voice boomed in my head. *"There will be no escape!"*

About the Authors

RODMAN PHILBRICK and LYNN HARNETT are the authors of another popular Apple Paperback series, The House on Cherry Street. Rodman Philbrick has written numerous mysteries and suspense stories for adults, and the much acclaimed young adult novels *Freak the Mighty* and *The Fire Pony*. Lynn Harnett is an award-winning journalist and a founding editor of *Kidwriters Monthly*. The husband-and-wife writing team divide their time between Kittery, Maine, and the Florida Keys.

Callie helped Star before... Now it's the ghost horse's turn to help her!

THE HAUNTED TRAIL

Phantom Rider
by Janni Lee Simner

*C*allie can't wait to go on a desert ride with her friends. But when the magical ghost horse, Star, suddenly appears, the other horses run away — leaving the entire group stranded in the desert during a torrential rainstorm! Can Callie convince an angry Star to save them from sure disaster?

Appearing soon at a bookstore near you.

PR1195